'Keep yer eyes peeled, Slugsy, I'm going in.'

The door squeaks, me heart hammers. No-one here, but you can feel his spirit. There's a scruffy old Bible and a book of poems, a notebook with funny writing, envelopes and 45p stamps tucked in a matchbox. On the floor's a portable stove with a weenchy saucepan balanced on top, and there's apples in a row and onions on a hook, and a shirt soaking in the plastic bucket Da uses to catch rainwater, and a toothbrush and paste on a shelf, and a big sharp knife smeared with jam.

Or maybe blood.

The grass can wait. I'm out of here.

spoofer rooney

Jonathan Kebbe

Corgi Yearling Books

SPOOFER ROONEY
A CORGI YEARLING BOOK 0440 864682

First publication in Great Britain

Corgi Yearling edition published 2002

1 3 5 7 9 10 8 6 4 2

Set in 11/15pt New Century Schoolbook by
Phoenix Typesetting, Ilkley, West Yorkshire

Corgi Yearling Books are published by Random House Children's Books,
61–63 Uxbridge Road, London W5 5SA,
a division of The Random House Group Ltd,
in Australia by Random House Australia (Pty) Ltd,
20 Alfred Street, Milsons Point, Sydney, NSW 2061, Australia,
in New Zealand by Random House New Zealand Ltd,
18 Poland Road, Glenfield, Auckland 10, New Zealand,
and in South Africa by Random House (Pty) Ltd,
Endulini, 5A Jubilee Road, Parktown 2193, South Africa

THE RANDOM HOUSE GROUP Limited Reg. No. 954009

A CIP catalogue record for this book is available from the British Library.

Printed and bound in Great Britain by
Cox & Wyman Ltd, Reading, Berkshire

*To Christine
(alias Operation Chaos)
thanks and love*

Hopper Rooney would like to say
thanks a million! to –
Breege Keenan
Rory O'Leary OFM
Marie Dillon
Colm, Sadhbh and Laoise Murray
Annie Eaton and Sue Cook
And me pals Natey Ayornu and Twene

The House of Giggling Drainpipes

There's someone living in our shed, and I don't know how to tell Da. He was always so big and strong, but the punch has gone out of him, the weight's walking off him, and the last thing he needs to know is someone's moved in with our lawn-mower.

Going to see him in hospital, me heart thumping.

Me auntie usually brings me – cos I live with me auntie – but today it's me mam, straight from the airport, all fussed and jumpy, trying to tell the cabbie the way, when he knows it and she doesn't. She doesn't live with us any more, she's been gone a couple of years, and I can't help throwing glances at me mam who I hardly know now.

It's a million years old this hospital, pointy windows and towers and big as a town with its own roads and shops and even a church, so you don't have far to go to die. Can't help thinking of all the patients who've snuffed it here, all them souls bumping round going, *Which way's Heaven?* Ambulances duck in and out with dark windows, nurses float by like ghosts; listen closely and you'll hear diseases giggling in the drainpipes, waiting to sneak in at night.

Hold tight to Mam, we're entering Dracula's castle – gloomy corridors, shifty-looking porters, demons dressed as doctors armed with needles, knives and axes, and everything reeking of disinfectant. I keep gripping me mam's hand, cos she hates hospitals and she's nervous about seeing Da. Closer to his ward, I can feel her holding back like a kid on her first day in school.

Suddenly we're here and she stops.

'You OK, Mam?'

'You go ahead.'

'But Mam, you said—'

'I know, love, but we don't want to go upsetting him, do we?' Making me take the flowers. 'Don't say I'm here.'

She's all smart and lovely. I was looking forward to seeing them together.

Mam and Da do be apart – but live together in me heart.

'I can't face it, love, I'm sorry,' she says. 'I'll wait here. After, we'll buy you something in your favourite toy shop – OK?'

I don't have a favourite toy shop any more, and I wish Mam wouldn't keep bribing me, cos

8

I always give in. If she said, *Be a love and jump in the river*, I'd do it.

The flowers are pinks and Sweet Williams and teeny roses wrapped in ferns. I set off holding them in front of me like a torch in a cave. Mam's right – seeing her would upset him. He misses her real bad, like when your dog's run over and you can't get used to it. He talks about her like she's going to walk in from the shops any second.

St Luke's Ward goes on and on and turns corners. Patients are six to a glassy room like fish in tanks. Can't remember where I found him last time, so it's hide-and-seek again, poking in and out of rooms looking for me daddy. I can't believe he's in this kip, he can't either. They don't even know what's wrong with him, something in his blood. I've nightmares about jellybeans growing into jellyfish in his veins.

There he is!

Me heart stops. He looks so scraggy in his skin and silly in his jim-jams, propped up on pillows with earphones on.

'Da . . . ? Da, it's me.'

Opens his eyes and tears off his phones, delighted to see me, and mortified cos he hates me seeing him like this. 'How you doing, kiddo – you look so big and grown up, I thought you were the consultant.'

9

'Here's flowers from Mam, Da – she's, um, not here – what's a consultant?'

'A super-duper doctor.'

'Thought you didn't like doctors.'

'These are the best in the business, son.'

'Did they find what's wrong with you?'

'Sit down, stop worrying, how's school? How's Uncle Maddy treating you? And where's your ma if she's not out there waiting for you?'

'I told you, Da, school's over for the summer.'

'And Uncle Maddy?'

'He's a gas, I really like him.'

Da gives me a crooked look.

'Honest, Da, he's real nice to me.'

'God help him if he lays a hand on you, Hopper. How's your ma?'

'Sends millions of kisses but couldn't make it – cos guess what! She got this call from What's-it Studios in Hollywood telling her to fly out and take over from Julia Roberts who slipped in the bath and twisted her uncle, I mean ankle.'

'So they phoned your ma, son.'

'And luckily she was in, Da.'

'So she's packing for Hollywood and you came all by yourself?'

Oops, what have I said? I'm not supposed to come on me own.

'Auntie Gracie dropped me off. She'll be back in a minute. And guess what, Da?'

'What, son?'

10

'You'll never believe the trouble I had getting in here – the whole place is guarded by giant cockroaches and GM-modified maggots.'

'No!'

'I had to blaze a way through with me armour-piercing water-pistol.'

'Never!'

'And guess what, Da?'

'What, son?'

'I passed this underground chamber crammed with skeletons of mams and kids and grannies, and you know who they are, Da?'

'Go on.'

'Visitors who got the visiting times wrong.'

'But you got through with your ma's flowers.'

'Do you like them?'

'Tell her they're beautiful, and maybe next time she'll bring them herself.'

'She's too slow, she'd never get past them maggots.'

We smile. Like old times.

'Tell us, Hopper, are you checking the house regularly?'

'Every two days.'

'And the garage?'

'Same. No worries.'

But the worry's in his eyes. *Rooney's Motor Repairs* was never closed for business before. Me grandad started it when dinosaurs roamed the Earth. It's only small, but it's a great little outfit and everybody thinks the world of Da. He can mend anything from a Lancia to a lawn-mower – blindfolded.

He looks out the window, wondering will he ever see his garage open again? He keeps sending out word he's looking for an experienced man to step into his shoes while he's sick, but it'll take someone special. He interviews them right here in the canteen. It's eating him up that he might have to sell his garage.

Every night I go to bed dreaming of ways I could save it.

With Da in hospital, I wish I could live with Mam, but she's gone and moved to England with her fancy feller. I say, 'Mam, can't I live with you for the summer?' and she goes, 'I'd love you to, but it's a bit tricky right now.'

'I promise to keep me room tidy and dig the garden and answer the door when Tom Cruise or Minnie Driver drop by for drinks.'

I like thinking of Mam as a film star, even if she only works for Age Concern.

'I know you'd be good, love, but Frank's a busy man and needs his peace and quiet.'

Mam's always right, and her fancy feller's real classy and can buy her everything Da couldn't, and they sit in London somewhere sipping cocktails on his terrace. Mam has people in when she wants to give a dinner party, and as soon as they're back from one trip, they're away on another. She promises to make it over one weekend a month, see friends, go shopping and take me out, but she never came in January or February, and missed out April and May.

I think about her feller and all the different things that could happen to him, like he answers his mobile too fast and the aerial goes through his brain, or the most venomous viper in the world swims up the toilet bowl on holiday and bites him on the bum.

Hopper Comes a Cropper

When Da went into hospital, me uncle came for me in his beat-up Volvo that looks like a hearse, flings me bag in the back like a binman and says, 'This wasn't my idea – we're living in a shoe-box as it is.'

He's a bit scary, Uncle Maddy, with his long white hair and greasy cowboy hat and the way he drives and rolls a ciggie at the same time, letting the car wander where it wants and only grabbing the wheel when a truck slices by like a cliff face. He's got Wild West posters in the bathroom and a stack of video Westerns you don't go near if you like living. He's handsome in a ship-wrecked kind of way, and breathes badly, like an outlaw with a bullet in his chest.

He looks at me like I'm a good-for-nothing, starts the engine and says, 'Any trouble, kid, and you're out. It's my way – or the highway!'

I think of me da in the big hospital, sleeping in a strange bed.

Their house is like ours: net curtains,

weenchy garden in front, skinny one out back and every room a white box.

Auntie Gracie gives me a hug. She's small and cuddly and smells of ciggies and perfume. Her painted eyes are like fake flowers and she speaks in a smoky growl.

'My! Hopper, you've taken a stretch! We'll be needing a step-ladder soon.'

She's right and I go red. I'm like me da's lettuces, bolting every which way. Anything you buy me today's too small tomorrow. Bus drivers don't believe I'm only twelve and punks in the street go, *Hey, Rambo! – No, not you, Scarecrow!* and me da takes me to buy shoes and can't believe the size the girl brings.

'Them's shovels, son, not feet, where the heck did you get them?'

'They just grew, Da.'

'You're very welcome, pet,' me auntie's saying, 'isn't he, Maddy?'

'Sure,' he wheezes, dropping me bag on the floor, 'only we're living in a matchbox as it is!'

'Don't mind him,' says Auntie, 'he wouldn't complain if Kylie Minogue moved in. Are you peckish, pet? We saved you a treat.'

'Don't get me wrong, Hopper.' Uncle Maddy slaps me back and nearly knocks me through the wall. 'You're me brother's boy, and I intend taking care of you like one of me own.'

That's what I'm afraid of.

15

'Come meet the lads,' says Auntie, and I follow her into the front room, where two older cousins I haven't seen in yonks are glued to *Who Wants to Be a Millionaire?* – which I hate cos it always makes Da think of Mam and how he might have held onto her if only he was loaded like her fancy feller.

'Say hello to your cousin Hopper, boys,' says Auntie.

Peach, the eldest, grunts without looking, and Ambrose peeks out at me from under a table like I'm from another planet, which I suppose I am.

Then in walks a girl I've never seen before – scarily pretty – and stares at me.

'Geri May, say hello to your cousin Hopper.'

I do know her. She's the daughter. Only thirteen, but all growed up.

'What are you looking at, you little gickball!' she says.

'Nothing.'

'You calling me nothing?'

'Mind your manners,' snaps Auntie, 'and fetch Hopper a cold drink.'

'Jeez, Ma, he's only in the door and I'm his skivvy already,' goes Geri May, and slinks out with a face on her like a burst ball.

'There, you see,' says Auntie, getting back to her ironing, 'you'll be grand with us.'

Geri May comes back with a glass of something fizzy and I think, *Oh no!* cos I've to watch

16

me intake of sugars and Es and stuff or all hell breaks loose.

'And cut him a big piece of cake with lashings of cream.'

'I'm OK thanks, Auntie, I like cake but it doesn't like me.'

It's no use, here it comes. Luckily it's only a meany scrap of cake and measly squirt of cream. And in any case, before it can reach me, Auntie Gracie leaves her ironing and snatches it away.

'Give it here, you big sulk!' she says, and walks out with it, and returns with a house-brick of cake drowned in cream. How do I tell her if I soak up too many naughty chemicals I'm liable to throw up or throw a fit – or both?

'Pamper yourself, pet, put some flesh on them bones,' says Auntie banging the dish down.

Me mouth waters – me brain goes *No! Hopper, don't!*

I take a sip of Coke – me tongue sizzles.

A nip of chocolate – me brain melts.

It'll take about four minutes. But it's worth it, dunking me brain in bubbles and goo.

Coke, choccy, Coke, choccy greased down with cream. I think of me da in hospital having stewed tea and a bickie.

Suddenly I notice Geri May's looking at me funny. I must have gone green. The little wreckers are in me blood, me brain's burning, the room's pitching like a ship, the coffee table hits me in the head and me sick hits the ceiling, or maybe the floor.

Open me eyes. They're all leaning over me, a last look before they nail the coffin.

'What's wrong with him, Ma?'

'Better call a doctor, Ma.'

That's the last time they give me Coke and cake.

scary Mary and the fruit Fairy

Weeks go by. I'm settling in nicely – like a gold-fish in a tank of piranhas. They're a funny lot, me cuzzies.

Peach is eighteen, taller than his da and good-looking. Next to Peach, I'm the geek at the ball. But then no girl would look at me if every boy in the world was wiped out by a virus. I think Peach hates me cos his da hates me and he worships his da. Uncle Maddy's horrible to him, and he still roars at his jokes. Peach blows his wages on clothes and girls and goes, 'Da, you got a couple o' quid to spare?'

'No. Get yerself a decent job.'

'I got one.'

'Call that decent after the hopes we had for you?'

'What's wrong with it?'

'You earn peanuts and stink of berries!'

Peach works in the greengrocer's and brings home bananas and bruised fruit on his clapped-out Yamaha he wishes was a Harley.

19

He's always chomping apples or some foreign fruit I never heard of, and if you get close to him he smells fruity, like he just stowed away in a boat-load of mangoes. His eyes shine and his skin's creamy and he's in and out the jacks faster than Michael Schumacher visiting the pits.

And he's not just pop-star handsome, he's a brainbox with a digital memory for mobile phone numbers and distant cousins' babies, and exactly how much Mrs So-and-so owes after she came in last week with no purse. With his head for figures he does the shop's accounts, and also checks Uncle Maddy's books after Auntie's messed them up. Before anyone's up he's away to work in a crisp shirt and trousers like he's off to serve toffs in the Shelbourne. When he's not in work he's swaggering out to meet some girl, in a cool summer suit with his hair slicked back and an earring. He lives for his job, but has his hobbies too – tropical fish and girls. The girls flit in and out of his life and never last; the fishies – big'uns and little'uns in all colours of the rainbow – live in his room, and I sneak in and watch them and read about them in a book he keeps.

Me, I share a room with Ambo, real name Ambrose. He's sixteen, looks ten and has the brain of a two-year-old. He's so pale and skinny he looks dead. He's got popping eyes and a pointy nose, and short spiky hair like a hedgehog shaved by a strimmer. He dribbles and twitches and doesn't say much. Actually, he doesn't say anything, so it's like sharing with a window dummy.

Peach is real protective. Anyone looks funny at Ambo in the street and Peach jumps in and goes, 'What are you looking at?' He's not happy about me sharing with Ambo – sticks his head round the door, points at me and goes, 'You upset our kid and you're mashed potatoes!'

Peach is mad and Ambo's away with the fairies, but Geri May's wildest of all, and scares the heebie-jeebies out of me with her black hair and fierce eyes and crazy clothes you'd say she'd borrowed from an older sister if she had one. She's thirteen but acts sixteen and looks at me like I just fell out me buggie.

She's got it in for me, and I steer clear of her like a mouse from the house moggy. But she's so pretty I can't help looking at her.

'What are you staring at, Shrimp?'

'Sorry?'

'I said, what you ogling at?'

'The spot on your chin.'

She goes pale and hunts for a mirror. 'If you're lying, I'll kill ye!'

I am lying, and I'm out the door!

I don't know why she hates me.

'Who took me shampoo, Hopper?' she yells at the top of the stairs.

Oops, I think I did.

21

Or, 'Ma! I'm freezing, the hot water's used up.'

'Hopper had a bath earlier, love.'

'He's always having baths and he never cleans up.'

What? I've had three splash-and-dash baths in three weeks, and I scrub the tub raw each time.

'He chews too loud, Ma,' she protests, 'never dries up proper, and his feet are too big.'

I hide me feet under the table, chew like a church mouse and wipe each dish like it's just been pulled from an archaeological dig.

Worst of all is running into her in the street.

'Get away over the road,' she goes, 'before me mates see you.'

I used to scuttle off out of sight, but now I say, 'Why should I?'

'Cos I don't hate meself enough to be seen with you – right?'

'You don't own the street.'

'I do if you're on it.'

'You're not my mother.'

She looks at me kind of sick and sorry, and I wish I hadn't said that.

Auntie Gracie's real nice, says things like, 'You all right, pet? Anything you need, pet? You must miss your daddy something fierce, pet.'

But Uncle Maddy scares me to death, the look in his eyes if you get it wrong, the way he shakes his fist at his kids when they cheek him, and bites the face off Auntie when she gets on his nerves.

Street Angel – House Devil, that's what they call das like him. Nice as pie in the village – Hitler at home.

He has an antiques shop – junk shop, Mam calls it. Lucky if he sells a mouldy Regency armchair or a cracked Wedgwood teapot a week, so you could say me auntie and uncle are poor. But Auntie always looks the lady going out at night in velvets and furs.

'It's a disgrace about your poor da,' she says, 'but we're lucky to have you, Hopper . . . aren't we, Maddy?'

'Mmm,' he says.

Uncle Maddy hates me da, and me da hates him. Years ago, Grandad left the garage to them both in his will, on condition Uncle Maddy gave up gambling. Uncle Maddy promised he was cured, and took over the garage with me da, and everything went smooth till Uncle snuck out one night with the takings and fluttered it all on a dead cert winner that lost. After that, Uncle had the itch worse than ever and kept sneaking out more money and chancing it on red-hot tips that came second or fell. When Da found out what was going on, he went mad and slung Uncle out, and they've not spoken a word since, not even *Merry Christmas, brother, drop dead.*

The Devil's Apprentice

I offer to help in the shop.

Uncle Maddy laughs. Auntie Gracie gives out to him, 'You should be pleased he wants to help.'

'What can he possibly do?'

'Sweep and dust,' says I, mad for Uncle to like me.

Uncle Maddy rolls his eyes. You'd think he was a brain surgeon and I was offering to sew up his patients.

We ride into town in his rusty hearse, Uncle cursing roadworks and traffic and anything that flies in without his permission.

'Poxy bee, get out of it!'

'It's a wasp, Uncle,' I try telling him. 'Da says it's best not to annoy them.'

'That right? And I suppose your da's an expert!'

Uncle's shop is in the old Liberties, snug between a pub and an oriental carpet shop. On the corner facing is a fenced-in pony chewing dandelions. A sign over the door squeaks in the wind saying *Rooney's Relics – established 1885*, which is only about a hundred years off the truth. The shop is stuffed with lamps and vases, armchairs and hatstands, brass coach-horns and coal buckets, cracked oil paintings, piggy-banks and chamber-pots, knives, forks, all sorts – the gloomiest collection you ever saw. Handy for a haunted house. You have to squeeze between tea trolleys and candlestands and a black leather sofa fit for Al Capone to find the poky office where Uncle Maddy chucks me a broom and says, 'When you're done sweeping, you can wash them dirty cups.'

'No problem!'

'Good man yourself,' he says, starting to see me potential. 'Make a good job and a few bob might find their way into your pocket.'

'It's OK, Uncle, this is fun.'

'I'm a fair man, Hopper. Play ball with me, and I'll scratch yours.'

While I work, I hear a customer come in with an oo-la-la accent. When I'm done sweeping and drying cups, Uncle's still haggling with yer man and trying not to choke him.

'I'm still find it a little bit expensive.'

'You're joking me, it's a steal!'

I look around. The office is a tip. If I kept me school desk like this, Miss Beatty would turn it upside down. What are these magazines doing here when they could be keeping them newspapers company over there? And yellow folders should be with yellow folders, blue 'uns with blue 'uns, and why not stack the catalogues alphabetically? And look at the state of that notice-board! Get to work, Hopper, make Uncle's day.

'Hopper!'

Running, 'Yes?'

Uncle's alone and in bad humour.

'One fiddling customer all morning. Fingers half the shop and buys nothing. How am I going to keep this ship off the rocks, you tell me that? Look at it, isn't it a beaut? Too expensive, my eye!'

'What is it?'

'What is it?' Amazed at me ignorance. 'A barometer. Predicts the weather.'

'Handy enough, I suppose,' says I, 'if you haven't a telly.'

'Work of art! Burr walnut with swash-turned pillars, about 1700, for Jessie's sake. Just cos it's not in perfect condition. Hell with it, I'm off to the bank. Keep the phone warm, Hopper, and I'll bring you back some chips. Lock the door and don't let a living soul cross the threshold.'

I lock the door as he goes and keep on tidying the office till a bell rings. Sounds like the door of the shop. It *is* the door of the shop!

Don't let a living soul cross the threshold.

I sneak out and look. A well-dressed feller's

26

peering in from the street. Sees me and calls through the letter-box, 'Would it be possible to look one more time at your beautiful *barrow-mayter*?'

What do I do? Say yes, and Uncle goes nuts for letting him in? Say no, and he goes nuts for losing a sale?

I open up. The customer comes in and gazes at the barometer like it's the bones of a saint.

'Real beaut, isn't it, mister?'

'Yes, but it's a little bit chipped,' he tut-tuts, 'and I would be surprising myself if it works.'

'Yeah, but you got to admire the twiddly bits. Must be about 1700, late summer, and it was working fine when we found it.'

'It was? Where?'

'San Francisco! Bargain-hunting across America we was when this earthquake ripped open the road – the street fell in, and when the dust settled, something was poking out the rubble and me uncle goes, *Look, a clock!* And I goes, *No, Uncle, a barometer*, and guess what! It said EARTHQUAKE COMING – WATCH OUT! So you see, it works!'

I can see he's impressed.

'Fascinating. How much, if you please?'

'How much did me uncle say?'

'Ah, interesting man, your uncle, all the time changing his mind.'

'Wait a sec,' says I, running to fetch Uncle's grubby register. He has his own pricing system, simple enough for Auntie if she's on her own. He sticks stars on everything, GOLD for *VERY DEAR* – *more than a hundred quid* – *check the inventory*; SILVER for *MODER-ATELY DEAR* – *rising to a hundred*; BLUE for *BARGAIN* – *thirty to fifty*; and YELLOW – *GOING FOR A SONG* – *pick a price!*

'What do you think, young man?'

Holy Hedgehogs! Where's the star? I turn the barometer round in me hand and there's nothing. Just my luck!

'I am happy to pay thirty-five,' says yer man.

Let me think. This item must have had a star, but what? Gold? Silver? – doubt it. Blue or Yellow then. If Blue and I sell it for Yellow, Uncle will bury me. Best go for Blue – and be clever, start high. What was Blue again?

'To be honest, sir, I'm looking for sixty.'

'Sixty? My wife would kill me.'

'Fifty-five?'

Yer man sighs and goes, 'Forty.'

'Forty! Me uncle would kill me.'

'All right, young man, my final offer – fifty.'

'Done.'

Can't wait to tell Uncle. Me first sale – fifty smackers off a fancy foreigner!

When Uncle Maddy gets back cursing the queues and the dipstick who served him, I say, 'Guess what, Uncle, that foreign feller came back desperate for the barometer. But I remembered what you said, not to let a living soul—'

'What! Don't tell me! I meant everyone else, not him!'

'It's OK, it's OK!' Fearing for me life. 'I took a chance.'

'You did?'

'He paid cash.'

'Cash?'

The word melts on Uncle's tongue. He puts his arm round me. I've a friend for life.

'You're a star, Hopper Rooney, I underestimated ye. Here's some fries! Where's the loot?'

I hand it over. He looks at them, five crisp new tenners.

'Where's the rest?'

'That's it, Uncle.'

'What do you mean, that's it? It was a gift at eighty.'

'B-but there was no star, and—'

'No star!' he goes, and looks around and drops to the floor, and there it is in the dust, a mangled smidgen of paper which only Uncle's pound coin eyes could have spotted. He picks it up and smoothes it out and what colour is it? – Silver!

'It's worth a hundred, numbskull, but I was willing to let it go for eighty!'

'I didn't see the star, Uncle, and he said his wife would kill him.'

'What's his wife got to do with it? I'm an antiques dealer, not a marriage counsellor. Fifty piffling quid! This is a business, not a boot sale,' he roars, coming apart like an old sofa. 'Why didn't you just put CLOSING DOWN SALE in the window! Better still, THIS IS YOUR LUCKY DAY — HELP YOURSELF!'

'I'm sorry, Uncle.'

'Sorry!' Fumbling for his tobacco. 'That's thirty quid down the swanny.'

'Sorry, Uncle,' shaking all over, 'but the other feller was getting heavy.'

'Enough for groceries, a tank of fuel, the shop's lekky bill! — What other feller?'

'Massive, he was, Uncle, with a patch on his eye and a T-shirt saying *Mike Tyson's a wimp*. Slaps me round and threatens to turn me into chewing gum . . .'

Uncle Maddy looks me over and shakes his head. 'Listen to him! One crazy yarn after another. And look at you! Your hair, your clothes. You're a disaster, Hopper, a raving scarecrow. Your mother was a brave woman.'

I feel like crawling into a hole.

'I don't believe in mercy-killing, son . . .' he goes, marching into the office to till the cash, 'but for you, Hopper, I'd make an exception.'

Any second now he's going to see the beautiful job I done, and when he does, his eyes'll hop out of his head.

I'm right, they do! And after he's finished

30

yelling at me, he doesn't speak to me for the rest of the day, nor all the way home in the hearse, where he gives out about me to Auntie.

'I'm sure he meant well,' she says.

'Meant well? Never in all me born days have I known such an eejit. Ask him to wash a few cups – he turns the place inside out. Leave him in charge of the shop – he gives it away! Next time your nephew wants to help, Grace, give him a pair of nail-clippers and let him trim the hedge.'

Slugs, Snakes and Spidermen

Me heart flip-flops each time I cycle over to the house – my house, me da's house – cos vandals hang round empty houses like vultures.

I'm even more worried what I might find in the shed.

On the way I pass our silent locked up garage – *Rooney's Motor Repairs* – body repairs, servicing, you name it, Da does it. Or did. The sign says CLOSED TEMPRALY DEW TO ILLNES. He was in pain when he wrote it. I knew he was bad cos he never shuts the garage and never gets sick. He likes to say, *Docs are quacks, and quacks are for ducks and I'm no ducks – so shucks!* He never takes pills either; *Pills are for weak wills – tablets for rabblits*. I can't get used to not finding him in his blue overalls with his head in a greased engine singing old songs – Sinatra, Eddie Cochrane, Elvis.

'Hi, Da.'

'Hi, son.'

'*Guess what? I just fought off a whole army of*

Bog Goblins and Vampire Spearmen between the church and Dempsey's Chemist.'

'I don't know how you do it, son.'

Any time I come in he smiles, and he nearly never shouts, and when he does he says sorry. He's got something seriously wrong with him, but they don't know what. It's not fair and I'm angry with yer Man upstairs.

I pedal on, whistling loudly, knees wacking the handlebars, not a care in the world – till I hit the new roundabout and get an eyeful of *Robert Barry Motors*, Da's local rival who's grabbing Da's customers. I can't look, all them cars stacked up in the yard.

Head down and pedal like the furies.

It's weird visiting your own house and not coming home. I turn into the street where I was born – boys and girls on walls or kicking balls and Mr Goggins from Number Forty-six flat on his back trying to fix the old banger he used to bring to Da.

Kids see me and look up.

'Hiya, Hop, you playing?'

I whistle and wave, Hopper the happy eejit, but sad inside cos Mam won't be there and will never be there again, not her perfume or her giggling fits or her sharp tongue. It's four weeks since she flew over and chickened out at the hospital, but it feels like years ago.

'Hiya, Hop, lend us yer bike?'

I pull a naff face and press the pace.

'You're mad, Rooney, get lost.'

Loony Rooney pedalling by, kissed the girls and cherry pie. Everybody's pal – nobody's friend.

'Hi, Hopper, how you doing?'

'Hi, Slugs.'

Slugs tries to act cool, but he follows you round like a pup if you let him, and I let him cos I'm lost without me besty mate Deano who's gone to Sligo with his family to get away from this kip. Me and Deano went everywhere, riding handlebars down Stoneybrack into the ditch.

'Need any help, Hopper?' begs Slugs.

'There's someone living in our shed. I'm going to check it out.'

'What, someone you don't know?'

Slugs is small and podgy with a little spitty voice like a mouth-organ from the pound shop. He's got hair the colour of ketchup and specs like ice cubes and he'll do anything for you.

'You can go in first if you like, Slugs.'

'The house?'

'The shed.'

We approach the house carefully. No broken panes, no tied-up hostages, no Snakeshead Bowmen in the bushes.

Don't worry, Da, I'll mind the house.

We wheel our bikes through the broken gate Da's been meaning to fix since the day I was born, when he hit it on the way to hospital with me mam going *Oooh! step on it, Eddie, I think it's coming!* She nearly had me there and then on the back seat – Da was going to call me Opel Rooney – but there was no traffic then, so they just about made it, and nearly had me in the lift in the Rotunda with Da going, *Hang on, Maggie my love, this is no place for a queen to drop her baby!*

Mrs Scully sees me and opens her front door. 'Is that you, Hopper?' she says suspiciously, like I might be planning to dig up her house. 'How are you, dear?'

'Fine, thanks, Mrs Scully.'

'Because that lawn of yours needs a good trim. And the beds are a disgrace. I'm looking out on a jungle.'

'I'm sorry, Mrs Scully, I been busy.'

'Doing what?'

'Planting onions with me auntie.'

'What, all week?'

'And watering them.'

'I'm sorry, but watering onions doesn't take a week.'

'You've not seen these ones, Mrs Scully. Big as basketballs and thirsty as pumpkins! So big they knocked down all her fences.'

'Oh, really! I've never known such a crackpot. No wonder your poor mother—' She stops herself. Too late. She may as well have stuck a fork in me heart. 'How is your mother nowadays, Hopper?'

'Fine, thanks, Mrs Scully.'

'And your father?'

'Grand. He'll be home any day.'

'Thanks be to God.'

'And how's Mr Scully, Mrs Scully?'

'Oh . . .' Sighs and looks to Heaven. 'Poor man can do nothing for himself.'

'We all have our crosses to bear, don't we, Mrs Scully?'

'Indeed we do, Hopper. I trust they bring you regularly to Mass?'

'Me auntie and uncle? All the time.'

I'm trying to imagine Uncle Maddy on his knees in church. Auntie Gracie takes Ambo to Mass, but Peach and Geri May just laugh, and the only time I seen Uncle join hands in prayer is when they're announcing the Lotto winners on telly.

'Oh, Mrs Scully, you've not seen nothing funny in the back garden, have you?'

'What sort of thing?'

'I just thought I saw – I mean – oh, it's OK.'

'You tidy up that garden, and tell your father I say a prayer for him every night,' she says closing her door.

'Thanks, Mrs Scully.'

I don't really like her. Her house is perfect, so's her garden, and she's always complaining about ours – like Da's got nothing else to do but paint windows and pull weeds. But when Mam left, Mrs Scully never said a kind thing, never

36

asked Da if he needed anything. It was like Mam never was. Me and Da watched telly pretending we had sniffles. Nobody knocked or said a word, just looked at us like we had Foot and Mouth.

'Ready?'

'Ready,' says Slugs.

Clutching me double-barrelled bicycle pump, I unlock the front door. The house is stuffy and creepy-quiet. Or is it? Listen close and you'll hear it whingeing: *Where you been? How can you leave me alone like this?*

'Sorry, house,' I whisper, 'Da's sick and they sent me away.'

'What's that?' says Slugs.

'The house wants to know when we're coming home.'

'When is your da coming home?'

'I don't know.'

'I'm sure he'll be OK, Hopper.'

'Me mam's bringing me to see him Friday. She's flying over Thursday, staying in a posh hotel. We're taking him out to dinner.'

'Will they let you?'

'Mam's meeting me in Bewley's at half-twelve. She'll have presents for me. She always does.'

I check the post. Flyers mostly: CARPET-CLEAN YOUR HOME IN 60 MINUTES! – QUIGLEY'S QUICK-FIX ROOF REPAIRS! – TREAT THE FAMILY AT TARA'S REAL ITALIAN PIZZA HOUSE! And this looks like a letter Da was expecting from the Revenue, and one from the insurance. I fold the letters in me pocket to take to hospital. Add the flyers to the heap on the stairs.

Lead the way up to me bedroom and we sneak up to the window. At the end of the garden stands the shed, not one of them boxy garden-centre jobs, a sound old shack like a midget's house or a one-car garage, leaking and rotting and wrapped in ivy.

Slugs and I gaze together. No sign of life. The ivy's so thick, you can only guess where the windows are, and who might be sitting inside looking out.

'The lock's been on the blink for years. Somebody just walked in.'

Mrs Scully's right, the grass and weeds are wild, but I'm not going near that shed if someone's home.

Slugs is looking round me room. I don't think he's seen it before. Since Mam left it's a bit basic, apart from the snake chart on the wall with its life-size vipers and boa constrictors, and a table covered with a sheet, which grabs Slugs's attention.

'What's under there?'

'A dangerous and mysterious world.'

Scratches his neck. 'Don't you have a computer?'

'No.'

Slugs spends half his life scoring goals and

38

zapping baddies on his PC, but I'm more the outdoor type, calling for mates and biking round Ballybriggan and shopping for Da – his rashers and Cream Crackers and grapefruit juice for vitamin C.

And nicking from shops.

When the mood takes me.

When I can't get Mam out me head.

'What are these?' says Slugs looking at a pile of magazines promising STUNNING NEW WAR GAMES KIT – TWO SEIGE CANNONS FOR THE PRICE OF ONE – LATEST ADVENTURES OF TRIBE-LORD KHARN AND THE QUEEN OF WRATH.

I open a deep drawer Mam used to fold me jumpers in, and take a peek at me legions of teeny Wasp Warriors and Storm Goblins sleeping off a battle.

Slugs, amazed, 'You play with these?'

I point to the secret table.

'Mind if I look?'

I shrug – be my guest – and he lifts a corner of the sheet which covers a wire frame Da made to protect me world of miniature hills and gullies, citadels, lakes and ruins.

'Wow!'

I'd love to bring them with me to Auntie Gracie's, but Ambo would wreck them, and Geri May would tease the face off me. Maybe I'll just bring a few Plumed Assassins and Dwarf Spidermen, hide them and take them out when it's quiet.

39

While Slugs goes 'Wow, this is so cool!' I open a smaller drawer and take a peek at me ill-gotten gains. I'm wanted all over the world and no wonder. The drawer's lined with gold bars lifted from the deepest vaults of the Bank of England. The British police are misty-eyed.

Actually, they're Cadbury's Crunchie bars nicked from Crazy Prices:

Crunchies missing here and there,
Crunchies missing everywhere.
Lord! another Crunchie theft,
Soon there'll be no Crunchies left!

'Wow, look at all them Crunchies!' goes Slugs.

'They're not Crunchies, they're solid gold disguised to look like Crunchies.'

Few outlaws have faced such odds as Spoofer Rooney, who robbed the rich and diddled the cops and caused his mammy years of heartache – and still she loved him.

They've put a price on Hopper's head,
A million quid I heard it said.
Bring him in alive or dead
And never let a tear be shed.

'Where d'you get them, Hopper?'

'I don't get them – I lift them in brilliantly masterminded raids.'

40

To be honest me crime sprees are not planned, they just happen when I'm upset.

'Don't you ever get caught?'

'Sometimes, if Alro Redlips is on.'

'Who's Alro Redlips?'

'Security.'

'Funny name for a security man.'

'It's a she, and her real name is Alro Redlips backwards.' Slugs can't work it out, so I tell him. 'Alro – Orla. Redlips – Spilder. Orla Spilder. She's caught me a few times. I'm on a last warning.'

'What do you do with them all?'

'Nothing.'

'Don't you ever eat one?'

'I can't eat that stuff. You can have one if you want.'

'You get fits and things,' he remembers.

'No, thanks. Anyway, I thought they weren't chocolate?'

'They're not – they're solid gold. Till you unwrap them and they turn into chocolate.'

He rides the highways of the night
On his trusty racing bike.
Lock your Crunchies up, you must,
Till Hopper Rooney bites the dust.

We tip-toe whispering down to the kitchen, scared the shed fiend's going to leap from a curtain and go, *Hee hee, brats for breakfast!*

41

The fridge hangs open and empty, except for beers Da keeps for his poker-night gang, who won't be needing them for a while.

I unbolt the back door. The garden's bright in the sun. I cover me eyes and brush against the forsythia Da planted to take the bare look off the bathroom extension, and a couple of snails clatter on the flags. I'm watching the shed, ready to run, listening for the smallest sound that isn't a bird or a car or Slugs sucking air, and then, as we break cover—

Yap-yap-yap . . .

Holy Horselips! We freeze together – staring at the shed.

Here he comes! A one-eyed ghoul! A giant! A drifter with a hammer! – bursting into the open!

Phew! Nothing.

Yap-yap-yap . . .

Oh no! It's Felix, Mrs Scully's pesky little floor mop running up and down her side of the fence like he thinks he's a wolfhound minding Madonna. He's only known me all his life but still goes bananas when he sees me, and won't stop unless Da gets him with the hose.

Yap-yap-yap . . .

I love animals, especially dogs and snakes, and couldn't hurt any of God's creatures, not even an ant or a wasp – they're all part of the plan, Da says – but somehow, when it comes to Mrs Scully's scabby little snapper, I can feel me finger on the trigger of the machine-gun.

Approach the shed. Either side of the door is a mucky window free of ivy. If I can get up the nerve, I'll take a peek.

Yap-yap-yap . . .

Deep breath – press me face to the glass.

He's there! Eye-patch and scraggy beard, sharpening his knives . . .

Heart thumping – no-one's there, far as I can tell in the gloom, and it looks the same as last time: one of them industrial pallets on the floor, a mattress of tied-together cardboard and a folded blanket.

Slugs, tucked in beside me, is shaking. 'Fancy playing round my place, Hops?'

I've just noticed something – how did I miss it? In the spare strip between the shed and the lane wall – rows of seedlings! Da was thinking about spuds there, but then got sick. Someone's growing carrots, radishes and I think that's garlic in our garden!

'I got to cut the grass,' I whisper boldly.

'Do you have to do it today?'

'A boy's got to do what a boy's got to do.' Felix the floor mop has finally stopped. I reach for the doorknob. 'Keep yer eyes peeled, Slugsy, I'm going in.'

The door squeaks, me heart hammers. No-one here, but you can feel his spirit. There's a scruffy old Bible and a book of poems, a note-book with funny writing, envelopes and 45p stamps tucked in a matchbox. On the floor's a portable stove with a weenchy saucepan balanced on top, and there's apples in a row and onions on a hook, and a shirt soaking in the plastic bucket Da uses to catch rainwater, and a toothbrush and paste on a shelf, and a big sharp knife smeared with jam.

Or maybe blood.

The grass can wait. I'm out of here.

Fruitcakes and Jigsaws

I won't say anything with Uncle Maddy
around, there's no telling how he'll react, but
first chance I get, I find Auntie alone, baking a
tart, the radio on.

'Auntie Gracie?'

'Yes, pet.'

'Can I talk to you a minute?'

'Course you can, pet.'

*'Mary in Celbridge – what did you want to say
about kids today?'*

*'Hello, Gerry, delighted to get through – I've a
girl and a boy and they never listen to a word I
say!'*

'I think there's something weird going on at
home, Auntie.'

'Who's going home, pet?'

'I think there could be someone living in our
shed, Auntie.'

'Might as well be talking to the wall, Gerry!'

'I know the feeling, Mary.'

'A foreigner, Auntie, living in me da's shed.'

'Your da said what, pet?'

I really like me Auntie Grace, but she's either a bit deaf, or one of them grown-ups who never listen.

'He didn't say anything, Auntie.'

'That's grand, love.'

'Only I think someone's moved into his shed.'

'Short of pulling their ears, Gerry, how do you get today's little horrors to listen?'

'What's in his shed, pet?'

'An escaped lion, or something, Auntie.'

'Is that right?'

'Or an axe murderer.'

'Sounds nice.'

I try telling Peach, but he's always rushing. It's like trying to stop a runaway train.

'Peach, can I talk to you?'

'No.'

'But Peach, it's real impor—'

'Can't keep pretty girls waiting!' he says, checking himself this way and that in the hall mirror. He's DJ-ing in some club tonight and he's manic as a box of monkeys.

'Don't tell your da, Peach!' Chasing him out the door. 'But I think there's someone living in our shed.'

'What's that?' he goes, climbing on his bike.

'A nutcase or an Astragoth or something.'

46

'What are you on about?' he goes, and then remembers it's me, Hopper the Hoaxer, Spoofer Rooney.

'Honest to God, Peach, I seen him – or rather I haven't, but I seen his butcher's knife and onions and foreign scribble . . .'

'Get out of it, ye mad twister,' he says, sticking his greased head in his helmet.

Brum-brum, and he's away in a whoosh of dust and fumes.

Thanks a bunch, cuz! I'm thinking, sticking me tongue out, which isn't fair of me, cos it's true, I am a mad twister. It used to drive poor Ma crazy. I come home and say, *Mam! I came first at school!* – a likely story. *Mam! Guess what, this feller stopped me in the street and says I can be in his movie!* Or, *Mam, you'll never guess, I just saw a robbery at Dempsey's Chemist!* That little outburst brings half the street round to the house, but once I start, I can't stop. *It was mad, Mam – they had wolf masks and shooters and I went diving for cover with lead whizzing over me head* . . . and then the doorbell rings and it's the Guards looking for a boy called Hopper Rooney.

'*Saw a hold-up, did you? Dempsey's Chemist?*'

'*Yes.*'

'*That's odd, cos there was no hold-up at Dempsey's chemist.*'

47

'*Oh, OK.*'

'*So why are you telling tales you saw one?*'

'*Cos I did.*'

'*You saw a hold-up that didn't happen – a virtual hold-up?*'

'*Yes.*'

'*A hold-up in your head.*'

'*Yes.*'

Everyone's laughing.

I knock on Geri May's door. No answer. Knock louder. Still nothing.

She's sitting at her computer with her headphones on – *tinty-tinty-tin*.

'Geri May!' I yell.

Swivels round. 'Did anyone say come in?'

'I've found books and clothes and stuff in me da's shed.'

'So?'

'And seeds planted in neat rows.'

'So?'

'It's not our things and we never planted nothing.'

'What you on about?'

'A foreign feller's moved into our shed.'

'What's a foreign feller doing in your shed?'

'I don't know.'

'Did you ask him?'

'I didn't see anyone.'

She looks at me like I got four heads, twists

up her face and says, 'I've met some fruitcakes in my time, but you take first prize.'

I don't think I handled that very well.

I may as well talk to the flowers, no-one believes a word I say.

Maybe I should run to the nearest cop shop and say, *Excuse me, I want to report someone living in our shed*, and they'll go, *Are you on your own?* And I'll go, *No, I'm living with relations.* And they'll go, *Why isn't one of them with you?* And I'll go, *Cos they don't believe me.* I'll be lucky if they don't clap me in jail.

So who do we try next? I find Ambrose in our room doing jigsaws.

'What's the story, Ambo?'

He tenses and carries on.

'Whoops, sorry,' say I, cos you don't disturb the master. No messing, Ambrose is the Jigsaw King – and you can only shake your head in wonder. His brains are scrambled, he's thick as a brick, he couldn't say *Help!* if his feet were on fire, but he can do a thousand-piece puzzle in ten minutes flat. He can even do them with the pictures worn off, just by the shapes, eyes glued and fingers flicking – makes you dizzy watching him, and today it's his favourite, an oldie-woldie automobile with oldie-woldie driver and passenger, or what's left of them after all the wear and tear.

Job done, eyes and fingers fall still.

'Ambo, guess what, there's a one-eyed giant living in me da's shed.'

He looks up, blankety-blank.

'Big as a house, Ambo.' I stretch up to show him. 'Big eye swimming with creepy-crawlies and big beard buzzing with bees – what do you think of that?'

He looks pleasantly surprised, tipping his head this way and that like someone's working his strings.

'Would you like to go see him?'

He looks at me kind of sad, like – *They won't let me.*

'No worries, Ambo, I'll talk to your ma.'

Pedalling to the shops for Auntie Gracie, I spot someone who looks like Geri May with a wacky hair-do – same cocky head and swaggery walk, and as she comes nearer, I see it is Geri May, all new and weird from the hairdresser. Maybe she'll believe me this time about the nut in the hut.

'What you doing here?' she says as usual, like it's her street.

'Me ma's flying over tonight!' I cry out.

She gives a little nod and keeps going. I swivel me bike and go after her.

'We're meeting in Bewley's in the morning and going to see me da.'

'He'll murder me,' she says.

'Who will, Geri May?'

'Me da, who d'you think?'

I see what she means. She's got gold streaks in her hair, and blue tag-on bits I think they call extensions.

'Why will he murder you? I mean, you look—'

'I look what?'

'Great! You look great. But, guess what? You know that strange man I was telling you about in me da's shed . . . ?' This isn't a good moment, but I can't stop . . . 'It's a maniac or something, with a butcher's knife and candle, so if you never hear from me again, it's cos he chopped me up in his cooking pot.'

'Let's hope it happens soon.'

'I'm not messing, there is someone!'

'You're mad, you are, Hopper Rooney.'

I watch her go.

You're mad, you are! That's the nicest thing she's ever said.

Trouble is, she didn't believe a word. No-one ever does. I've this reputation for stopping at nothing to get a laugh.

Like one day last term, instead of saying, *Sorry I'm late, me da asked me to run to the shop*, I said, *Sorry I'm late, miss, but leaving the house I was jumped by a robber who said, 'Give us yer wheels, you little Scuzzy!' and I said, 'I like me bike – so take a hike!' and took off like the wind, miss, with half the dogs in Ballybriggan after me, and just when I'm*

51

*thinking, Phew, that was close! a white limo
slinks alongside me and crime boss Jack
McCase points a Magnum in me face – not the
ice-cream, miss, the real thing – and says, 'I
warned you not to cross me, Rooney,' and me
belly turned to jelly, miss, cos Smacker Jack's
no prankster gangster – he'd sell his granny for
a Mars Bar. But even with a shooter in me
hooter I never wobbled, miss, I smacked him so
hard with that atlas you lent me, his head fell
off and rolled across the road going, 'Oi, give us
me body back!'*

The class rolled in the aisles, even Miss
Beatty had to smile. I'm hopeless at Maths and
Science, I can't draw to save me life, I always
say the wrong thing, lose everything anyone
gives me, can't be fagged with football or
running, and when I offer to tidy up, I leave a
room worse than it was. All I'm any good at is
reading aloud and spinning a yarn, and Miss
Beatty even gives it for homework, says, 'I
want you all to write a fantastic excuse for
being late, and we'll act them out tomorrow.'

Even a sap like me can swing the curriculum.

Returning from the shops, I catch sight of
Uncle Maddy stumbling from the house like a
gunslinger from a saloon, flinging himself in
his Volvo and driving off in a huff.

Auntie Gracie's half laughing, half crying in

the kitchen. Geri May's been banished to the darkest iceflows of Astragothia – her bedroom.

'Flipped his lid, Hopper.'

'Cos of her hair-do, Auntie?'

'He had her in bits, and she never cries.'

'What did you think of it, Auntie?'

'Getting tears out of that girl's like getting milk from a plank.' Lights a ciggy and sips her tea.

'I think it suits her, Auntie. Will I go up and tell her?'

'Tell her what, pet?'

'Tell her she looks great.'

'Grounded her for a month. *You'll be in every day by five,* he said, and that's when she cracked, cos she lives for her mates.'

'Will I go up and see her, Auntie?'

'See who, love?'

'Me cousin Geri May.'

'Life's tough enough without turning every tea leaf into a dung hill.'

'Did I tell you, Auntie, there's a hobo or a Communist or something in our shed?'

'Is that right, pet?'

'You think I should tell Da tomorrow?'

'Tell him what, pet?'

'The red in the shed, Auntie – what if he's dangerous?'

'Dangerous? Don't you worry,' she says, twisting out her ciggy, 'your Uncle Maddy won't lay a hand on you while I'm still breathing.'

'Thanks, Auntie.'

Standing at her door, practising. *Just want to say sorry your da gave you such a hard time, Geri May – and by the way I think your hair's great.* Knock. 'Geri May?' Louder, 'Can I come in?'

No answer.

The room's dim with closed curtains and the glow of her computer screen, and stinks of turps. She's sitting on the floor with headphones on, painting her nails blue to match her extensions.

'Just want to say sorry—'

'Why, what you done now?' Tearing off a headphone.

'No, I mean—'

'You've not touched me new shampoo?'

'I mean sorry about—'

'Why can't anyone leave anything alone in this house? Jeezusss!'

'I never touched your—'

'That's not any old gunk, it's expensive stuff the stars use and it's wasted on the likes of you, so get yer own, right? Here, have some choccy!' she says, jumping up and coming at me with a stick of Toblerone. 'I saved it 'specially for you – go on, put some meat on that skeleton!'

Backing out the room, 'Thanks, Geri May, but I can't eat choccy – remember?'

Sure I remember, her smile says. *How could anyone forget?*

'Go on – treat yerself!' she says, driving me down the stairs and out the door, where I bolt like a rat.

Face to Face with Alro Redlips

It's Friday at last, I'm seeing Mam and Da. Hardly any sleep last night thinking of Mam flying in. Meeting her in an hour or two and me nerves are wrecked. What if they miss out a bus or two? Or the bus breaks down, or there's roadworks or a pile-up? Or they've moved Da to another hospital, or superbugs have closed the ward . . . ?

I keep peeking in the drawer where I've hid me loyal legions, feel them forming a circle round me, Goblins and Spidermen protecting their wounded Chief from the Tribes of Gloom.

Geri May's on washing up, me drying.

'Hopper, will ye wake up and shift them flaming dishes – we'll be here till Christmas!'

Watching the clock. Nine fifty-five . . . Nine fifty-seven . . . Mam will be in town ducking in and out her favourite shops.

Auntie's going to walk me to the bus. I'm to meet Mam at twelve-thirty. The bus takes half an hour – call it forty with the traffic. Add ten minutes to get to the bus stop – twenty in case Auntie meets someone and starts yakking. Another five for the bus to come – call it ten, so that's forty, plus twenty, plus ten makes . . .

God knows! Leave around eleven-fifteen to be safe. Say eleven.

'Hopper Rooney – will you concentrate!'

Or even half-ten. Better an hour early than an hour late. Can always check out the jugglers and fire-eaters in Temple Bar, or visit the War Games Workshop in Liffey Street.

'Auntie Gracie – can we leave a bit sooner?'

The phone's ringing.

'What's that, pet?' she says putting down her magazine and specs to answer it.

'Can we leave a bit sooner, Auntie – like now?'

'With you in a sec, pet.'

I'm so jizzed up I can hardly stand still. Mam will arrive looking great and smelling lovely. I'll wait behind a potted tree so I can see her step in off the street. She'll have her hands full of bags from all the posh shops, and a bag for me – special bickies with no naughty chemicals, fancy toys I don't play with any more and stuff to wear I'd hate from anyone else, but I'll wear all week for her.

Geri May's fingernails float in the suds like blue fish. She's stopped banging wet dishes into the rack. She's looking round – something's up.

57

'I'm sure he'll understand,' Auntie's saying, 'just be very disappointed . . . not to worry, we're taking good care of him . . . not a bit, he's a great boy . . . yes and you too, Maggie, God bless.'

Me heart freezes. I can feel their eyes on me. I turn back to me dishes, flimsy cups and glasses lying on top of each other in the rack – carefully picking them over so as not to endanger any survivors there might be under the rubble.

'Hopper, come here a sec, pet.'

There could be babies and old folks under here – you have to work real slow, one saucer at a time, one egg cup, taking care not to shift anything – you'd be amazed how long people can survive.

'Hopper love – that was your mam . . .'

You have to listen for the smallest cry, and then carry on, one cup, one glass at a time . . .

'Calling from England, pet – she's really sorry – something important at work . . .'

Me eyes sting, but I won't give in, not in front of Geri May.

'You all right, pet? We could go to the video shop later, if you like, choose something nice?'

'Can I visit Da on me own for once, Auntie?'

'She's a busy bee, your mam, isn't she? – always on the go.'

'Is it OK if I go anyway, Auntie?'

'I'd say she's good at her job, very professional.'

'Da's expecting me,' says I, accidentally bumping the draining rack.

A cup slips, a family dies.

'So, is that OK, Auntie – if I go on me own?'

'I'm sure she'll be over soon, pet.'

'Ma! Are you listening, or what?' Geri May bursts out.

'What, love?'

'Hopper's only asked the same question five hundred and fifty-four times!'

'What question's that, pet?'

'Is it OK if I go anyway? See me da?'

'On your own?'

'It's only into town, Auntie.'

'And out again the other side.'

'Will you come then, Auntie?'

'Not today. It's tourist time, they're flocking into the shop. Bills to pay, pet. Make hay while the sun shines.'

It's all gone quiet. Too much time has passed – no sound below. We're all exhausted, specialist teams from Switzerland, Israel, Jupiter. I turn away, wiping the sweat from me brow. What more can we do?

'Why don't I take him?' says Geri May, pulling the plug and lashing in green slime to scrub the sink.

'Blasted flies!' Auntie's saying, shaking a can and going after them like a mad woman.

'I said, why don't I go with him, Ma – and will

you leave off that disgusting spray – there's only one flippin' fly!'

Auntie doesn't hear – she's stumbling about spraying fire like Queen Thespa vanquishing the Dorks of Glum.

'Open another window, Auntie,' I'm saying, 'and it'll come in one and go out the other.'

'MAM! Are you listening? I want to go with Hopper, OK?'

Auntie smiles sadly. 'Have you forgotten you're to be in by five?'

'We'll be back by then easy!'

'And you're too young to mind Hopper.'

'Jeeez, Ma, I'm thirteen!'

'Yes, and still a child and I'll thank you to leave Jesus out of it.'

Flying along, wind in me eyes and spits of rain.

Ride me bike fast as I can,
Dennis the Menace and Desperate Dan.
Flush me worries down the pan,
I will always love me mam.

Swing by the garage, stop a sec at the gate, rattle the padlock and check the shutters, everything eerily quiet, only litter scratching round in the yard and a leaking pipe.

Press the pace, monkey-face! while you still got the nerve to cut Da's grass. Faster, faster! Stamp these streets to powder, smash the world to bits. I want to scream, start a tidal wave, break me heart in Mam's lap. Silly thoughts, soppy talk, cop onto yerself, Hopper, think of something funny, like the time you offered to clean out Miss Beatty's gerbil cage, and they got out and ran in the staff room with half the teachers hopping on chairs and the rest on their knees trying to catch them.

The rain blows in me eyes, the road slippy-slides under me wheels. Whistle and sing – not a bother.

It's raining, it's pouring,
Me granny is snoring.
Swigs a barrel
Of beer a day
And can't get up in the morning.

I've a slow puncture in me back wheel and I keep having to stop and pump. Here comes the church, the Shell garage, the shops – and Crazy Prices, tempting me with all that gold, daring me.

MAM! WHY COULDN'T YOU MAKE IT?

Leave me horse untied for a quick getaway and stroll in. Aisles nearly empty, shoppers half asleep.

Eyes peeled for Alro Redlips, I go looking for me gold, and find it, where it always is – gone! So scared of me they've moved it.

Ah! There she is, Miss Redlips, dark blue

61

uniform and red hair tied in a burning pony-tail, chatting to a check-out girl.

Deeper into the evil empire, down the milk and yoghurt aisle and west into crisps and nibbles and aha! there it is – me precious gold.

Whoops – there she is again, the Wolfslayer, looking straight at me.

Backtrack quick, past fruit and veg to take cover behind the blood-soaked carcasses of the meat counter.

All clear, turn south into noodles and pasta and close on me treasure with the moon behind me.

Hell's bells! It's her again! Hands behind her back, pretending she isn't watching.

Move quickly now, down the Vale of Washing-up Liquid and into the Canyon of Sauces and Ketchup.

It's a smart move – but she's clocked it. Prepare for battle.

Me heart's drumming so hard I'm afraid it's going to burst me chest and dance in the aisles – *blub-blub-blub*.

The gold bars sway nearer in the glare of enemy shields, me knees wobble under the weight of so much armour. I reach and grab. Will one bar satisfy? I don't think so, grab another! Um, maybe not – put it back. On the other hand – blast! Dropped it.

One on the floor and one in me paw! Run!

No, walk, cool as a cat, the Crunchie wrapper

sticky in me hot hand. The whole thing's going to melt before I hit the street.

Oho! Redlips is on the move – I feel her in me slipstream, eyes burning holes in me helmet.

The automatic doors part like Hell's gates – I feel a hand on me shoulder.

'Hello, Hopper.'

Turn. 'Hello, miss. We meet again.'

'We certainly do.'

I'm captured – taken prisoner, through the Valley of Floor Polish and Shoe Wax to the little door marked STAFF ONLY.

Face to face with my victorious adversary, her painted claws in me shoulder.

'Now, Hopper, have you got a receipt for that Crunchie?'

'No, miss.'

'Did you pay for it?'

'No, miss.'

'Would you like to give it back then?'

I hand over the billion-dollar bar.

'And would you like to pay for it now, Hopper?'

'I don't have nothing on me, miss.'

'OK, Hopper, I'm going to let you go again. But this is your last, last, very last warning.'

'Thanks, miss.'

She watches me go, through the store into the open.

Me wounded steed's still in the rack. I pump

up his gammy leg and wheel away with rain
cooling me cheeks, singing as I go.

> *It's raining, it's pouring,*
> *Me mammy's in mourning,*
> *Did me in with a rolling pin*
> *And now me soul is soaring.*

See a Boat Race – Take It Easy

Turn into my street. The rain's stopped, and sun's lashing the roofs and setting the road on fire. Can't be fagged to pump again, so ride wibble-wobble through smoke and flames and cries of the wounded.

The street's all midday and snoozy, and there's Mr Goggins still working on his heap, head in the engine like an eejit snapped by a crocodile. Da keeps telling him to scrap it. It's not a car, it's a dog's dinner. Mr Goggins is too loyal to turn to any of Da's rivals, so he's fixing it himself. Ambo'd make a better job of it.

The house looks peaceful, resting up like a dog in the sun. And no sign of Mrs Scully – great!

Wait! Curtains twitching, she's at the window. Quick! Through the gate and open the door before she can—

'That you, Hopper?'

No, it's the Pope! 'Oh, hello, Mrs Scully.'

'Have you come to do the grass?'

'Yes, Mrs Scully.'

'Good boy. You made a lovely job of the beds.'

Beds? What's she talking about?

Let meself in. The house is having another sulk.

You again! Nicer places to stay, have we?

'Sorry, house, I miss you too.'

Run up to me room and look out the window. The shed's shut, no sign of life, thanks be to Jaysus – but me heart's beating fast and I'm suddenly tired. Mam cancelling and Alro Redlips being so nice – it's doing me head in.

The grass is about ten feet higher than it was the other day. Elephants could be in there playing hopscotch.

Oh my God! I see what Mrs Scully means. The beds – the flower beds, they're all neat and weeded and beautiful!

Who did it? And all so spruced up.

Wide awake again, creep downstairs, unlock a million bolts on the back door and slink smoothly into the garden, ready to drop to one knee and blow anyone away with me bicycle pump. No sign of Floor Mop Felix. Tip-toe over wet grass to the shed and take a peek. Everything looks the same, pens and paper on the table, blanket folded on the cardboard bed – except the basin that was soaking a shirt is turned on its side, and – jumping jellybeans! the same shirt's drying on a bit of twine strung out between the shed and the back wall, where somebody's radishes and carrots are doing fine.

Jeepers! What do I do now? Sneak away and pray I'll be braver tomorrow – or cut the grass fast as I can and run?

Yes, that's what we'll do. Come on! Into the shed, eyes shut to everything but the mower – the two mowers as it happens: the whirry one that screams like a banshee, and the roly-poly that belonged to Grandad and goes *clickety-clack, clickety-clack*. The banshee's quicker, but you have to plug it in in the kitchen and I'm always falling over the cable and yanking it out the socket. And it's so loud you can hear it in Hell, and anyone could sneak up. But it is quicker.

Will I risk it?

Wait! What's that? Just as I'm dragging the banshee out the shed, getting it stuck and unstuck and stuck again, and knocking spades and hoes over and falling over them trying to pick them up – someone in the back lane, humming to himself.

That's cool – no law against humming.

Me heart stops to listen for the hummer to go on his way – please!

He doesn't. He stops on the far side of the wall. What's he doing? He's not? He is! Climbing over!

His shadow leaps the wall and lands in Mam's hydrangeas. His face, neck and hands are dark as wood. He looks just like an African.

He *is* an African! – a hop and a skip from where
I've turned to stone in the shed door. He's fit
and strong and young, and he's watching Mrs
Scully's house, afraid to be seen. Now he's
moving, pushing flowers from his face, and
Holy Spokes! He's turning this way, looking
straight at me—

Murder in his eyes!

Me belly flips over, I think I'm going to poo
me pants. He has me in his spell, should've
said me prayers last night – sorry, God, won't
happen again. Me life's over – I remember Mam
hugging me when I was a little snot, Da lifting
me on his shoulders – the African's coming for
me, me brain's leaving home – hands by his side
ready to strike, eyes big as billiard balls, fingers
closing round me scrawny neck, squeezing the
life out of me. Bye-bye, world, bye-bye, Hopper
– nice knowing ye. His face is close, his voice
African – soft with a joke in it – something like
'*Jiwa who me – see a boat race.*'

Blackout.

Someone has me by the shoulders, puts a
chair under me bum and wets me face with
a handkerchief. I wake like Sleeping Beauty
after a hundred years, look into his dark eyes,
and feel the heat of Africa on me skin. He's
looking at me kind of funny.

'Why are you afraid?' he whispers, patting
me face with a towel. 'Breathe deep and slow –
deep and slow.'

He's speaking English, posh with an African accent.

'*Jiwa who me, see a boat race*, relax, my friend, what's your name?'

Might be an idea to answer, but me heart's stuck in me throat. He's the first African I've seen up close. He's about Peach's age, with white teeth and skin like chocolate gone smooth in the sun, and hair neat and tight as a rug.

'This is your house, I suppose?' he says, like I just caught him nicking me bike. He's whispering and keeping an eye out.

You're right, I want to say, *and if you know what's good for you, you'll hop right back over that wall.*

'Is your mummy in?'

'No.'

'Your daddy?'

'Yes! And he's big as a house and hard as hell and the last feller who crossed him wound up in hospital with three broken legs.'

'I better speak to him nicely then. My name is Kofi Amankwa. Friends call me Fifi. What's yours?'

He has a name. He has friends. He's dressed nicely in a creamy-coloured shirt and track-suity trousers, and he's not going to hurt me.

Me belly unwinds, me heart drops back into place.

'Hopper.'

'I didn't quite catch that?'

'Hopper. H, O, double-P, E, R.'

'Sorry to give you a fright, Hopper. I have no right to be here. Let me talk to one of your parents.'

'Me da's in hospital and Mam's in England. She was supposed to fly over yesterday, but couldn't make it.'

'I'm sorry to hear it. Did your father have an accident?'

'He's sick. They're doing tests.'

He makes a kind of sad *hmm* sound, and then a little clickety-click with his tongue like he's thinking.

'If you don't mind,' says I, 'I got a question.'

'Good! I like questions,' he says – but suddenly, music! posh music, tumty-tumty-tum, coming from his pocket. He digs out a mobile and answers it well away from the door.

'Mrs Quincy! How are you? . . . Yes of course . . . Oh, it's a bit late for seeds, better I buy plants . . . There's a space around the cucumbers . . . No trouble, I'll be with you about three o'clock . . . Yes! or four o'clock African time . . . Me too, bye-bye.' He puts his phone away and giggles like a girl. 'It's a little joke we have. She always expects me to be late, and of course I never am. She wants to grow courgettes. Do you like courgettes, Hopper?'

'I don't think so, and you didn't hear me question.'

'Ask it, then.'

'What you doing in our shed?'

'Ah.' He smiles like a naughty boy.

'There's laws in this country against squatting.'

'In mine too.'

'You can go to prison.'

'Yes.'

'Solitary confinement.'

'Oh dear, I wouldn't like that, I'm a sociable person.'

His accent's a gas – oh *deeer*, and sociable *pair-son*.

'Your accent's funny, mister.'

'You think so?'

'And how come you speak English?'

'My parents sent me to a good school. Every lesson is taught in English. Also English is everybody's common language in my country, where we have hundreds of languages. Any more questions?'

He's laughing at me, but not nasty.

'Was it you did all that weeding, mister?'

'Every morning at home I rise at six to tend the garden and cycle to school, where we tend the gardens before class, and again after school, and once more when I get home. I would have done your lawn, but was afraid to make noise. Would you care for a cup of tea?'

'No thanks. Where you from anyway?'

'Ghana. You know where that is?'

'Africa?'

'Africa's a continent. If I ask where you from, do you say Europe?'

'No way. I say Ballybriggan, or Ireland.'

'You can fit Europe in Africa's suitcase, Hopper, Ireland in Africa's pocket. Ghana's in West Africa, next to Togo and the Ivory Coast, just down the road from Nigeria and Cameroon.'

'Yeah, but you're still dodging me question.'

'And you know why?'

'You don't want to answer it?'

'I don't discuss this with strangers.'

'What d'you mean?'

'My name is not Mister.'

'I can't remember your name. I was scared you was going to kill me, and years from now they'd find me bones in the roses.'

I'm still shaking. He smiles and spreads his hands. 'You still afraid of me? We've known each other at least five minutes.' His hands are amazing, dark brown with pinky palms. 'Before I came to this country, Hopper,' he says, facing me on an upside-down bucket, 'I had a good life and promising future. Now I'm living in a garden shed. It's important to look after your self-respect – you understand?'

'Not really.'

'Don't worry.' He laughs, like I'm two and a half. 'Soon as I've had a nice cup of tea, I'll be on my way.'

'You mean—?'

'Yes.'

He fills his teeny saucepan from a bottle, and puts it on to boil. 'Are you sure you won't have a cup, after your shock?'

'No thanks. Where will you go?'

'I'll find something. It's not a problem.'

'How did you find this shed?'

'I was sick after I came to this country. It was raining hard one night and I said to myself, Kofi, you better find some shelter. The church was shut and my prayers didn't break the locks. I approached houses with no lights on till I found your shed unlocked. Next day no-one came. Next day the same, and the next. I guessed you were away.'

'Why sheds? I mean, don't they have proper places?'

'Yes, but you have to be in when they tell you, and eat what they give you. They don't let you work, they give you pocket money. Mrs Quincy kindly offered me lodgings in her fine house in Chapelizod, with a view over the river to the Phoenix Park. That would have been nice.'

'Why don't you say yes?'

'Her son said no.'

'Doesn't he like you?'

'It's a bit more complicated.'

Suddenly I twig. 'You're one of them refugees, mister, aren't you? The telly and papers is always going on about Simon seekers

73

flooding the country. Are you one of them?'

The question puts the sting on him. He looks itchy.

'I told you, my name's not Mister, and this is a personal question.'

He switches out the gas – he's gone off the tea – and pulls out an old suitcase. 'Excuse me, I have things to do.'

He's packing note-pads, onions and socks, a pocket radio he had somewhere, T-shirts, a cup and saucer wrapped in newspaper . . .

I don't feel great about this.

'Your first name's something like hot chocolate.'

Laughs! 'Hot chocolate? *Your dinner's on the table, Hot Chocolate!*' he calls out, taking his mammy off.

'Or tea or coffee or something. That's it! Your name's Coffee.'

'Kofi,' he corrects me.

'Kofi,' says I, with the O you get in *oh, no* and *blow*.

'And a nickname like a girl's name – Trixie, or something.'

'*Wake up, Trixie, time for school! – Yes, Mumma!*' he answers in a deep voice.

'It's not Trixie, then?'

'Fifi.'

I'm getting used to his handsome kind of cheeky face. His skin's dark and mysterious as trees at night, and smooth as icing on a cake –

74

except for a scar on one cheek under the eye. You don't see Africans round here, only in town waiting for buses or carrying babies slung like broken arms.

'Will I call you Fifi, then?'

'That depends.'

'On what?'

'Friends call me Fifi.'

Doesn't he want me to be his friend? Cos it feels like we're nearly friends already.

'Why can't we be friends? We've known each other at least ten minutes! And in any case I'm running out of friends since me besty mate Deano scooted off to Sligo, and me nexty besty mate Franny Walsh went to the Algarve on his holliers, and all I've left is Slugs, who's looking forward to meeting you, by the way . . . once they let him out of jail.'

'Jail? A friend of yours?'

'Well what d'you expect if you go shooting dead the Queen of England's favourite yapping corgi?'

He stops and looks at me. 'How old is your friend?'

'Twelve, like me.'

'And he shot the Queen's . . . ?'

'No, not really.'

'But you just . . .'

'It just comes out – when I'm nervous.'

'You don't have to be nervous of me – as long as I can trust you.'

'You can trust me – Fifi.'

'Thank you, Hopper, but you must tell no-one about me . . . not even the Queen of England.'

'Cross me heart. Except me Auntie Gracie, she's sound. If that's OK?'

Shaking his head sadly, 'It's best you have nothing to do with me. The authorities are looking for me. I should have accepted the kind hospitality of your government, but I felt – what's the word? Restricted. Here I cook what I like, and come and go when I want, and answer to no-one but God and the stars. I've done wrong, but I'm not a criminal.'

'So are you a refugee?'

'Not yet. I'm still a minor.'

'A miner?'

'Not that kind of miner. A child in the eyes of the law. In six months I'll be eighteen, and then they interview me again. For now I'm seeking asylum.'

'What is asylum?'

'Shelter from danger.'

'How come—? I mean, what made you? – I mean, was there a war or something?'

A kind of jitter goes through him like an electric charge.

'I have to go now and buy Mrs Quincy's courgettes and plant them before her son comes by after work.'

'Why, is he giving you a hard time?'

'He doesn't like me near his mother. He wants to go to the police.'

'What's stopping him?'

'I fixed his car. That stopped him. For now.'

He kneels on his case to shut it. 'Don't worry, I'll be back later to tidy up. Nice to meet you, Hopper,' shaking me hand. '*Nantiyie* – walk well, goodbye. I hope your father gets better.'

He looks out at Mrs Scully's windows, and leaps into the hydrangeas. Flings his suitcase over the wall and follows it over.

I hear him go on his way humming, swinging his suitcase, like he's back on some dusty road in Africa – I mean, Ghana.

His steps fade, but his hand's still cool in mine.

Time to cut the grass.

 Moses to the
Rescue

In the middle of cutting the grass, the banshee
stops screaming and I can hear me ears
working again. I stopped it meself. I'm staring
into space, thinking about Fifi.

I'm sad, happy and mixed up. I just made a
new friend – and lost him. Ought to contact *The
Guinness Book of Records*, shortest friendship
section. Wait till I tell Da I met an African
called Kofi, or Fifi, and guess what? – he was
living in our shed, honest, Da! No spoofing. But
it's OK, he's gone now.

'Hopper?' Someone calling.

It's Mrs Scully over the fence. I don't want to
see her.

'Hopper! Wake up, what's wrong with you?'

'Oh hello, Mrs Scully.'

'Come round the minute you're done, you
hear?'

Big trouble! She's seen Fifi, she's going to
grill me and call the cops. I'm sweating,
finishing Da's grass slow as I can, over and over

78

the same spots till the lawn's bald as a bunch of monks. Panicking.

But when I go round, polishing me lies, she stuffs cash in me hand – not the stacks of loot I got for bumping off Smacker Jack, just two pound fifty to be a good boy and cut her grass, cos her Ronny's too sick and she's not so lively herself.

So I cut her grass and trim the edges with Felix going nuts indoors like a fly in a window. Grab the loot and run to the shed to put away the banshee and stop! – and stare at Fifi's things, his bed and mini-stove and shirt still fluttering out of sight, and can't help wondering what Mam would have said, and Da would have done. Slung Fifi out, or let him stay? Or – who knows, invited him to use the spare room in the house?

I close the shed, lock up the house and get on me bike with me head rattling, cos I'm worried I done wrong and it's twisting me up I don't know where Fifi's going to sleep the night.

The sun's shining overhead, but Holy Spokes! Look at that big black sky growing like an oil slick behind me. Better ride hard or get blitzed. Sun's hot in me face, air's cold on me neck and I know I ought to go like the clappers, but something's holding me back and it's not the leaky tyre, it's something Fifi said, and I can't think what.

Riding through Ballybriggan with the end of

the world over me shoulder, I'm proud I got Da
his shed back – ashamed too, and I can't fit the
feelings together, like salt and custard. I'm
pedalling and getting nowhere like in a dream,
trying to stay ahead of the storm, but not caring
if it splits me in two, stopping every few
minutes to pump the tyre with the first spits of
rain on me head, and then, just as I get home –
if you can call Auntie and Uncle's place home
– lightning flashes in me face like water in a hot
pan, the sky goes BANG! and the rain comes
like needles, and I run to help Auntie get in her
washing, all the while thinking of Fifi looking
up at the same sky as he plants his courgettes
and wonders where he's going to sleep tonight.

Me heart's sick. What have I done?

Nothing! Only asked a squatter for a shed
back. What was I supposed to do?

The storm bends the tree and lashes the
window and I can't sleep for hearing his funny
voice going, *Why are you afraid? Breathe slow
and deep*. Where is he now? Trying church
doors? Kipping under a bridge with his case for
a pillow and one eye peeled for cut-throats?

*My name's not Mister, and that's a personal
question.*

Suddenly I'm sitting up in the dark, busting
with excitement. Didn't he say he'd be back to
tidy up? Maybe with the storm he'll leave it till
morning. If I get over early I'll catch him!

But there's something else he said that's still bothering me, or exciting me. I'm not sure, I can't remember what it was – only that it was important. Think! I should've listened closer, but I never do, do I, Mam? *That's half your trouble*, says Miss Beatty – *head in the clouds.*

Sleep at last and straight into weird dreams about Fifi, the new teacher in our school shoved out to a potting-shed classroom where we're crammed so tight the room shakes and breaks its moorings and sweeps out to sea, bobbing and weaving with dolphins and fairground rides, and when I wake—

Me mind's a blank.

Can't remember a thing about yesterday – only long ago things like Mam bringing me for me first haircut, and Da unscrewing the side wheels off me kiddy bike to make a big boy's bike, and the time Gran found a Viking coin in Sandycove that turned out to be an old English ha'penny . . .

Then it hits me – Fifi!

Me heart jumps out of bed and I'm at the window looking out at the rain that's stopped and turned to sunny clouds.

It's half-seven and Ambo's already up in his half-noony on the floor doing a jigsaw of sail boats racing on a rough sea like in me dream, and I'm getting dressed like a loon, tripping over meself, getting stuck in the same trouser leg and falling over Ambo going, 'Sorry – sorry – sorry!'

For the moment I've nearly forgot me mam cancelling yesterday, and all I can think about is Fifi, and whatever it was he said yesterday that's still knocking on the windows of me thick brain.

Auntie Gracie's wandering round in her dressing-gown.

'See you, Auntie!'

'No good mornings this morning, pet?'

'Sorry, Auntie, good morning – did you sleep well?'

'Like a log, pet. What you having for breakfast?'

'I'll save it, Auntie. Got to see the house is OK.'

'What about a slice of toast to keep you going, pet?' she calls, but I'm long gone, pedalling crazy, stopping every few minutes to pump and pray, Please, God, let Fifi be there tidying up or asleep or picking carrots before he goes. I got to tell him I didn't mean to sling him out and he can stay long as he likes till he's fixed up. You're not telling me it's part of your big plan to let an African far from home kip in the rain? Answer me prayer, Boss, and I promise to go to Mass with Auntie for the next three Sundays and drag Geri May along by the hair.

Geri May on her knees in church, Lord, what's that worth?

Our street's quiet, kids still in bed or crawling down to breakfast. There's Mr Goggins in his car scratching his head with the engine open, and all of a sudden I remember what it was Fifi said that's tormenting me. The woman he works for, her son was going to tell the cops – but Fifi *fixed his car*.

Fixed his car! That's what he said.

Does that mean Fifi just kind of got it going – or can he really fix cars? And if he does, could he fix Da's customers' cars?

WOULDN'T THAT BE COOL! Hopper Rooney finds the feller who saves his daddy's garage!

Me heart's doing somersaults, I'm so jizzed up I can hardly get the keys in the front door. Mrs Scully's calling out the window, but I'm not hearing, not today, not when there's half a chance of catching Fifi and saving Da's business.

'Hopper? Hopper! Come here to me – don't go out back whatever you do, there's someone out there!'

There is? Must be Fifi! Thank you, God!

But wait! If she's seen him, I got to warn him – quick!

Charging down the hall – no time to look at post or say hello to the house, fumbling with keys and bolts and dive out the back door. The sun's in me eyes. Where is he?

Run to the shed. Look in.

'Fifi . . .?'

He's gone. Everything's gone. The pallet, the

tiny stove, the lot. Everything neat, and tidier than ever it was. The washing line and shirt gone too.

I'm in shock – like the guy in the desert in one of Uncle Maddy's movies who nicks the other geyser's water pouch and leaves him to die, only to find next day, under the scorching sun, the stolen pouch is punctured, there's not a drop left and he's done for.

Uncle Maddy's right. I'm a complete eejit. I can't look God in the eye. I tried to make a deal – let me have Fifi and I'll give you Geri May! He didn't buy it.

Worm, you cast my servant Kofi into darkness!

There's a whole in me heart. I sit on the bucket Fifi sat on and hold me head. When Mam left I cried for an hour and that was it. After me first visit to Da in hospital I cried for another hour, and that was it too. I'm not going to cry now. It's me own stupid fault – and so what? I only knew him a few minutes. He was trespassing and I was nice about it. He found this shed, he'll find another. He probably fixed Mrs Quincy's son's motor by mistake. It's not my problem – leave me alone!

Anyway, Fifi didn't think bad of me. He'll be Prime Minister of Ghana one day and he'll fly me out to do his lawn.

Yap-yap-yap!

'Hopper? Hopper!'

I don't believe it! It's Floor Mop and Mrs Moan. Hysterical – 'Where are you? . . . Felix, get down, boy! That's enough! . . . Hopper? Is that you?'

No! It's Frankenstein's Monster. I want to yell and march out and lift her and Felix over the fence and crack their heads like coconuts.

'There you are, child! There was a man just now – I've called the Guards twice! A *coloured* man! Stealing things out of your shed and throwing them over the wall!'

She's all fired up, smoke coming out of her ears.

'I can't understand it, they should have been here by now – get down, Felix! – and you get back inside, Hopper.'

Jumpin' jacks, Fifi'll think it was me who called them.

'Get back inside yourself,' goes a man's voice – Mr Scully in his jim-jams, wandering into the garden like a ghost.

Now I hear them, over Floor Mop's yapping – sirens!

'About time too!' goes Mrs Scully.

Here they come, whooping and wailing so loud I half expect police cars to leap the roofs and land on the lawn. Brakes scream, sirens die, I think that's Mrs Scully's front door.

'Quick, Ronny!' she screeches. 'Oh never mind!' And goes herself. I hope she trips over her face.

They're running out into Mrs Scully's garden, cops in uniform or jeans and some sprinting down the back lane, and Floor Mop's gone completely mental – why doesn't somebody shoot him? One of the snoops is trying to question Mrs Scully, but she's too busy going, 'It's an absolute disgrace letting them over here to do what they like. We're not safe in our own beds! Oh do shut up, Felix!'

She's holding her poor heart. Mercy! A coloured man in her neighbour's shed seen legging it with – um, a pallet and some cardboard.

The Guards look tense. Two of them jump the fence onto my side.

'You on your own, son?' says a big bloke in a leather jacket with a crook's meany face.

Nod me head.

'Did you see anyone?'

Shake me head.

Someone's asking Mrs Scully to describe the thief and she's squealing *'Black as the Ace of Spades!'* with Felix throwing in his bit, so everyone's having to shout.

'Let's see what's missing,' says Crook Face marching me into the shed.

'It's all here,' says I much too quick.

'How d'you know?' says the other cop, who's dressed neat and talks soft.

'I know every hook and cobweb in here,' says me.

86

'Take your time, lad, look around,' says Softy.

You bet! I'm thinking. Spin it out, give Fifi time to get away, and up and down the shed I go, pointing left and right, 'One mower, two mowers . . . one rake with half its teeth missing . . . one long-handled hoe, one short-handled coal shovel . . . one light fork for me and one heavy-as-hell one for me da . . . one pair of rusty clippers you couldn't cut a pack of cards with, never mind a hedge . . . one old spade and one new spade – we used to have five, but neighbours borrowed them during the gravediggers' strike to bury grans and pets and misbehaving snots in the back garden . . .'

They're swapping looks, like coppers on telly.

'Nothing missing then?' says Softy. 'You sure about that?'

'I told you, I nearly live in here. Me and me da go in for prizes – second last year in the All Ireland Juiciest Carrot contest, and this year we're in the play-offs for the Biggest Beetroot in the World competition, which is going to be tough, cos we're up against growers from Goa and farmers from Jarmers and—'

'What's this?' goes Softy.

He's found something. A dusty old book. No!

'It's a Bible,' says I. 'It's mine.'

'Yours?' goes Crook Face, grabs it and opens it.

'It was me grandad's. He left it me.'

'What's it doing here?'

'I'm studying for the priesthood. Me mam's real proud. I sit in here between showers. There's some real good bits, like today I was reading how Moses climbed Mount Cyanide to fetch the Ten Commanders and was on his way to Canada when he snuffed it.'

'It's got Kofi writ here – K-O-F-I,' says Crook Face.

'Sorry?'

'Who's Kofi?'

Blood flies to me cheeks. Me heart's going like a drum. 'Um, let's have a look?'

He gives it me and I look at 'Kofi' pencilled inside the cover and wait for me brain to come up with something while they stare at me, arms folded.

Come on, Hopper . . . come on . . . ah! Here comes something.

Laughing, 'That's not Kofi, that's coffee! Mam ran right out of coffee last week and told me to remind her to get some, cos she's got a brain like an old shoe and I jotted it in me Bible so I wouldn't forget, cos I've a cloth head too, mister, I'm always forgetting me homework, me bus fare, me American Express card . . .'

'Yeah, and your spelling's not up to much either.'

They laugh. I look gutted. 'What d'you mean?'

'What's your name, son?' says Softy.

'Hopper.'

88

'Well, Hopper, I'm sure your mammy doesn't drink coffee with a K and an I!'

'No, she takes it with milk and a bickie.'

Softy's looking peeved. I'm pushing me luck. He nods over in Mrs Scully's direction. 'Your neighbour says she saw a coloured man. Is she, um, you know . . . ?' Rolls his eyes a bit.

'Is she what?'

'Is she all there?'

'All where, mister?'

'You know, the full shilling?'

'The what?'

'Are all her lights on? Does your neighbour imagine things?'

'All the time.'

'You saying she's mad, son?'

'I've never known such a crackpot.'

They've given up searching the lanes and they're gone. Mrs Scully can't believe it.

'Where are the helicopters – the sniffer dogs? I won't get a wink's sleep tonight.'

I nod and look worried. Then I go inside and start locking up. Now it's over I'm trembling so hard my heart could start a landslide. Fifi's got clean away and I'm faint with relief and sick with sorrow. I'll never see him again, and Da's garage is done for and Da will die pining for it.

Then, just as I'm turning to go, me eye catches something out in the garden, moving in the hydrangeas.

Fifi?

I'm scuffling with bolts again, fast as me fingers'll go, sneaking into the sun like a thief, praying Mrs Scully's not looking till I'm safely . . .

. . . in the shed – 'Fifi!'

He spins round, big eyes. 'Hopper! You trying to scare me? You win!'

'There was cops everywhere!'

'I know.'

'Looking for you.'

'I thought so,' he says, tapping a loose panel round a cracked window pane.

'It wasn't me, it was me neighbour. What you doing?'

'In my hurry I forgot this,' he goes, digging out an envelope and waving it. 'My daddy never hurries. He wouldn't have left all this money behind.'

'Where is your daddy?'

'I don't know, Hopper.'

'Something happened . . . ?'

'Yes.' He holds his breath and I shut up.

'It wasn't me grassed you up, Fifi.'

'I'm sorry?'

'I didn't tell on you, honest to God.'

'I believe you, *jiwa who me – see a boat race*.'

'And you don't have to go, you can stay long as you like – only what's all this *jiwa who me, see-a-boat-race* business?'

'I thought a bright boy like you would speak

90

at least one African language. It's not *see a boat race . . .*' He digs out a little pad and scribbles – *Si abotre*. 'Pronounced *si-abotray* – take it easy. You say it.'

'*Si abotre.*'

'Good! And *ji wuahumi* – relax!'

'*Ji wuahumi!*'

'There! You're learning Twi. Now I got to go.'

'But I'm telling you you can stay.'

'That's very kind, but it's not safe now for me or you.'

'Wait! I got a question.'

'What is it?'

He's cool but nervous and I'm holding him up.

'You said you fixed yer man's car.'

'What man?'

'The courgette lady's son.'

Laughs. 'I really got to go.'

'Tell us about it – please.'

Fifi sighs, takes a peek out the door and talks fast over his shoulder. 'Rick is his name, nice chap, good suits and big BMW, very protective of his mother, keeps telling her to get rid of me, because I represent trouble and she could go to prison – all baloony.'

'Baloney.'

'Baloney, thank you.' Turns to me. 'He insisted to see my papers. "I'm pretty sure you're illegal," he says. "I'm perfectly legal," I reply, "and I am not obliged to show you anything." But he has me worried, he can make

91

big trouble for me because I'm not as legal as I should be and I know they want to find me. So while he argues with his mother about calling the police, I slip out and open his engine and make a minor but essential – what's the word? – adjustment.'

'What sort of adjustment?'

'One or two wires – and back to my pruning. Later he gives me a dirty look and says, "You haven't heard the last of this," and jumps in his car. *Brrrum-brrrum-brrrum* – nothing. I wander over to take a look. He says, "What would you know about cars?" and I explain I worked for my father's friend, who owns the biggest garage in Ghana.'

'That true, Fifi?'

'Of course. Holidays and weekends in his garage in Accra handling all the best people's cars, even government cars. "No! Out of the question! I'm late as it is," he says and calls a taxi. After he's gone, I have a very pleasant lunch with Mrs Quincy as usual. We discuss the wonders of the world while we walk to put flowers on her husband's grave, and I go back to work, forgetting all about the BMW.'

'Then what?'

'Suddenly, late afternoon in the greenhouse, a taxi! – "*Run, Kofi!*"'

'You ran away?'

'No, to the car, where Rick finds me scratching my head in the engine and laughs. "*Still at it! The great mechanic!*" He thinks it's very funny, me working five hours on his car. "*Just as well we're not sending you our government's cars! Ha, ha, ha! Full marks for effort, but I think we better call the professionals, don't you?*" "Wait!" I say. "Try it now." He shakes his head and laughs, gets in, turns the key, and—'

'It works perfect!' I laugh out loud. 'He must have felt a right prat.'

'*Shhh!*'

'Sorry. I hope you charged him for fixing it.'

'He wanted to pay. I said, "Out of the question! Let's shake hands instead." We shook hands, but he wasn't happy and said, "*Don't think you're safe now, because you're not.*" So you see, Hopper, I live day to day, praying my birthday arrives before my friend Rick picks up the phone to the police.'

'And after your birthday, they'll let you stay?'

'I hope so – if they accept my story. Because if they send me home . . .' He stops, his eyes big with fear.

Me heart flips. 'Will you tell me your story sometime, Fifi?'

'Sometime, perhaps. Now I really must—'

'Hang on! Where did you stay in the storm last night?'

'I have a confession, Hopper. *Here.*'

'Good. Wish I'd known. I couldn't sleep. But listen, I got a better idea for tonight. Guess what these are for?' says I, jingling the keys on me belt.

'I give up.'

'A giant balloon in Stephen's Green!'

'Giant balloon?'

'Handy enough in the city centre, fifty quid if you want to rent her, fifty more if you scratch or dent her – what d'you reckon to that?'

'I think you're pulling my leg.'

'You're right. They're for me da's garage. You'll be comfy there. There's an old fridge and a kettle. What d'you say?'

He does that clickety-clickety thinking thing with his tongue again.

'You've done enough for me already.'

'You joking me? I sent you packing, I nearly got you caught. I'll meet you there at, um – six! OK?'

'You're a good boy, Hopper.'

Me heart's flying and I'm dying to ask him, would he consider having a crack at saving me da's garage. 'Fifi, before you go . . . ?'

'Not now, Hopper.'

'It's real important.'

'Later. Where's the garage?'

'Five minutes away, you can't miss it.' I give him directions and we shake hands. 'Can I tell me Auntie about you? You can trust her.'

'Be careful.'

Stink Bombs and Fruitcakes

Pedalling happy, pedalling scared, me tyre shredding and the wheel kicking up sparks. Fifi's free! Fifi's in danger. He's going to say yes – he's going to say no. Auntie Gracie's got to help – if I can get her to listen.

When I get back, screeching to a skiddy halt, Peach and Uncle Maddy – with Ambo the Expert snooping over their shoulders – are working on Uncle's Volvo which has packed up again, and I sneak by into the kitchen going, 'Auntie! Guess what?' only to find Geri May setting the table.

'What – what is it?'

'Nothing.'

'What d'you mean, nothing?'

'Not telling you.'

'What you hiding, ye big sly?'

'It's a secret.'

'Oh yeah?' she says, and pulls a packet of Penguins from the bickie tin, peels one and pins me against the cooker with it. 'You going to talk,

Shrimp? Or am I going to make you eat this?'

The smell of choccy and Geri May's fancy soap fills me nose and makes me queasy-weasy.

'Spill the beans — or bite the bullet.'

I've me mouth zipped tight, but I'm starting to drool and ready to bite when just in time in walks Auntie Gracie with a ton of groceries.

'Geri May! What do you think you're—?'

'Look at him, Ma! He's skin and bones.'

'And making him ill's going to help? Leave him alone.'

'Sorry, Ma.'

'Don't sorry me, sorry Hopper.'

'Sorreee,' she goes, and waggles the Penguin behind Auntie's back to let me know she's not finished with me.

The others are still working on the car, so we sit down without them. Too jizzed for food, I'm playing pool with fork and peas.

'You got to eat, pet,' says Auntie, 'the flesh is falling off you.'

'And mind your flipping knees,' goes Geri May, 'you're making the table jump!'

'Sorry.'

'You will be.'

'You OK, pet?' says Auntie. 'You've been twitchy as a whippet for days. Is it your mam, pet? She couldn't help it, she really wanted to come.'

'It's not that, Ma,' says Geri May. 'He's got a

secret just for you. Work away!' she goes, hands over ears like she's not listening.

I don't care if she hears. I want her to hear, want her to see there's more to me than a puking scarecrow.

'I seen him, Auntie! The mystery man in me da's shed.'

'You what, pet?'

Geri May's nearly gagging trying not to laugh. Ha, ha! Loopy Rooney again.

'But I've met him, Auntie!' says I, sick of playing the joker. 'He's an African Simon seeker with a scar under one eye and he was real kind when I fainted, but Mrs Scully called the Guards, and they grabbed and grilled me, and I never said a word . . .'

It's not just Geri May swallowing giggles. Peach and Uncle are cracking up in the hall listening to me.

'What's so funny?' says Auntie.

Peach and Uncle Maddy tumble in together like pickled punks to wash their icky hands in the sink.

'Don't listen to him, Ma,' goes Peach. 'He's mad.'

Even Ambo wanders in and looks at me like he never dreamed he'd meet someone loopier than himself.

'I keep telling you, Gracie, he needs a doctor,' hisses Uncle Maddy, like I'm deaf as well as an eejit.

'A shrink more like,' says Peach, 'with a few hundred years to spare.'

'Don't get me wrong, Gracie, he's a nice kid,' says Uncle, 'but wired to the moon since his mam left.'

'Later, Maddy, please, not in front of the boy.'

'You need help, cuz,' says Peach to me face. 'You're a fruitcake with added nuts.'

I feel like planting stink bombs in Uncle's shop, fireworks in Peach's fuel tank. Feel better just imagining it – Uncle holding his nose and flinging open windows, Peach going up in smoke as he rides away.

'He's not as mad as he looks,' says Geri May.

I lift me eyes. Was that a compliment?

'And he just might be telling the truth,' says Auntie.

'Right! We'll see about this once and for all,' says Uncle, and picks up the phone and calls Directory Enquiries to get Mrs Scully's number, and nails her first time and says, 'Sorry to bother you, it's Hopper's uncle. The boy's banging on about a man in the garden shed, and we're wondering is this another instance of his scrambled brain, or—?'

'No! I seen him with my own eyes, black as tar and running off with half the shed, so he was . . .'

All of us can hear her, and Uncle has to hold the phone away to save his brains.

'*The police lost him, Mr Rooney, can you believe it! Saints preserve us, I never thought I'd see this country overrun with coloureds and criminals . . .*'

'We'll be like England next,' says Uncle. 'Muggings and spicy food and no-one speaking the same language. But listen here, Mrs Scully, you see that scoundrel again, forget the Guards – call me, I'll take care of him . . . Bye-bye now . . . same to you . . . God bless.'

'Me and all, I'll fix him,' goes Peach the hero, flexing his pretty face.

'See!' goes Geri May. 'Hopper was telling it straight all along, wasn't he, Mam?'

'Game, set and mashed potatoes to Hopper!' says Auntie Gracie. 'Time some of us listened to him a bit more, and gave out to him a bit less. One or two apologies wouldn't go astray.'

'I hold up me hands,' says Uncle, holding up his hands like the bad guy pretending to be the good guy.

'Yeah, well,' says Peach.

Geri May gives a snort like a ratty horse. 'Was that an apology?' she says, looking first at her da and then her brother. 'I didn't hear no sorries.'

'That's as sorry as I'm gonna get,' says Uncle, drying his big scabby hands.

'After the sickening things you two just said?'

'And as much cheek as I'll take from me own daughter.'

'Should be ashamed, the pair of youse!' goes Geri May, wrinkling her nose in disgust.

'Ah, shut it, bonehead,' says Peach.

'You shut it, pussball!'

'That's enough!' says Auntie.

'Tell her, Grace,' says Uncle, 'or I'll take me hand to her.'

'You will not.'

'I will.'

'You won't!'

'You gonna stop me?' he roars, leaning over her.

'Over my dead body,' says Auntie, getting out of her seat, five-feet-nothing eye to eye with the monster.

Nobody moves. Uncle Maddy's wheezing.

'Foo-kay,' says Ambrose, breaking the spell.

'What was that, honey?' says Auntie.

Uncle drops hacking into a chair and digs out his tobacco. Nothing like a smoke to lift a cough.

'You'll be the death of me, the lot of youse,' he says.

'Great!' whispers Geri May.

'I'm getting sick of these rows,' says Auntie.

'Exactly!' says Uncle. 'What's wrong with youse all?'

'And I don't like you airing your godless views on the phone,' goes Auntie. 'Half our

100

relations live in England and it's a lovely place and they're blessed having so many of God's family under one roof.'

Peach and Uncle Maddy swap grins across the table, like she's nuts but you have to love her.

Ambo again. 'Foo-kay.'

'Once more, hon?' says Auntie.

'Foo-kay, foo-kay!' he says, delighted with himself.

'Good boy, hon, but we're not quite with you.'

Ambo blows a big sigh. He's said enough for one day, it's not his fault everyone's thick.

'Daft as a brush, my little man,' giggles Uncle, lighting up a skinny ciggy and snapping open a cold beer for himself and one for Peach.

'Our kid's not daft,' says Geri May. 'I heard what he said.' Peach laughs at her. Geri May spits like a cat. 'Just cos I know Ambo and you don't.'

'Listen to her!' Peach hoots. 'Ambo's official interpreter!'

Geri May sticks out the longest tongue you ever saw, longer than them lizards that snap up flies.

'What did you say, hon?' says Auntie. 'One more time for Mammy.'

'He said fruitcake – didn't you, Ambo?' says Geri May. 'Loud and clear, if anyone bothered to listen.'

101

Everyone looks at Ambrose, who's staring into space.

'And he don't mean Hopper,' says Geri May.

'Must mean you, Peach,' says Uncle Maddy.

'No, he means you, Da,' says Peach.

'Fruitcakes the pair of youse,' says Auntie. 'The whole lot of youse! A house full of fruit-cakes!' she goes, and everyone laughs and tucks into their grub.

Me heart winds down. I hate fighting.

'So what was he like, Hip-hop, this African feller?' whispers Geri May.

'She's wrong, he never stole,' I whisper back. 'He's seventeen and lost his family and had nowhere to sleep.'

'Shouldn't talk to strangers, pet,' says Auntie.

'Especially scumbag refugees,' says Uncle Maddy.

'Could have got your throat cut,' says Peach.

How to Catch a Cobra

Eejit! You said too much. You promised Fifi.
It's nearly five – I'm meeting him at six.
Patching me tyre in the sun with me heart
galloping, waiting for everyone to go so I can
raid the kitchen for Fifi's supper.

It's Peach's day off and he's running out to
catch the pet shop for a new pump for his fish
tank before it shuts. Uncle and Auntie are
dressed to drive to an auction to buy more junk
for the shop, and taking Ambo with them,
attached to Auntie's wrist with a toddler's
lead so he can't do a runner. Any minute
now . . .

All quiet, 'cept for Geri May's earphones
going *jinkety-jink* upstairs. She's in disgusting
humour every day at this hour, cos her mates
are out having fun and she's stuck in with me.

Here goes, into the kitchen, diving into the
presses and fridge and finding apples, bickies,
slice of tart, half a packet of Corny Flakes

and— Holy Cow! Geri May in the doorway, hands on hips looking lasers at me.

'What you think you're doing?'

'Tidying.'

'Thieving more like. You know where that African is, don't you, and you're nicking our stuff to feed him, right?'

'He's got no home, Geri May, and—'

'We're not yer flaming welfare.'

'I know but—'

'And we're not exactly millionaires either.'

'Please don't tell.'

'You're in big trouble.'

'You won't tell, will you?'

She steps back into the hall and checks her face for spots in the mirror. Then she's back and says, 'What's he like, this African? Weren't you scared?'

'I don't think I'd better tell you.'

'What d'you mean?'

'Don't want to give you nightmares.'

'Try me.'

'Promise you won't tell?'

'Promise!'

'Seven feet tall.'

'What!'

'And starkers, except for a tea towel.'

'No!'

'Eyes like coals and muscles like caulies, and a pointy spear he flung at Mrs Scully after she called the cops. Split her skull in two with guts flying like confetti and her poxy dog running for cover.'

She's not pleased. 'You're crazing me, Hopper Rooney!' she goes, and marches up the stairs, and marches right back down again, like the Grand Old Duke of York with blue extensions, and fixes me with those laser eyes and says, 'I'll make a deal with you.'

'You will?'

'You don't tell I'm slipping out to see me mates, and I'll pretend I never saw you nicking food.'

She winks at me, and a warm feeling goes through me. I think she's starting to hate me a little bit less.

'Geri May?' I call after her.

'What?'

'Do you think we might have some bedding to spare?'

'We're not flaming Oxfam,' she goes, slamming the front door.

On me way out with bags of goodies, I stop in the mirror to see how I look these days. I hate Geri May thinking me ugly, and I keep hoping for signs of improvement, a trace of Ronan What's-it or Tom Cruise creeping into me face. But all I see scowling back is a skinny sap with a big nose. When God made me cousins ('cepting Ambo, of course) he was in flying form; he must have been in a right mood when he made me.

The coast is clear. I stuff me saddle-bags with grub and set off through fields of smoke and ash on me new wheel.

Come on, come on, you're late!

Me head's fizzing with plans. Fifi's going to do it, I know he is. Da will be so happy – Mam amazed!

Who are you spoofin', Hopper? Fifi's not going to say yes. Anyway, what if he's not there? What if he's been nicked? What if he's been hit by a meteorite? What if . . .?

Cutting through the graveyard, kicking up a pink blizzard of blossom, I hear the church bell wind itself up and go *PANG! – PANG! – PANG!* It's going to strike six times, I know it, and it does! How am I late today of all days?

When I get there, pounding and panting – no sign of him.

No sign of anything. It's like the garage never lived.

I drop me bike and sit on the kerb. I like this spot, tucked away off the big roaring road to the airport, a cobbled street no-one hardly goes except to bring their cars. There's a few old houses with old folks living there since the Ark. Da's good to them cos of all the noise and stink, and any cars they bring in – he never asks who owns them and fixes them cut price. There's a walled-in yard topped with barbed wire all round the garage for customers' cars. It's empty now, full of stones and glass and bashed cans rolling round.

I'm being watched – a gull the size of an albatross on the roof. Maybe it is an albatross. Or a vulture. I'll wait and I'll wait and they'll find me in a month or so, a pile a bones behind the bins, picked clean.

The church strikes far away in the summer air, half-six.

Fifi, where are you? Did the cops get you? Did you miss home and hop on a plane?

Me heart tick-tocks. Six thirty-one, six thirty-two, he's not coming and I'm getting cold. The gull takes off, bored. This is a ghost town. The garage will never reopen, the air will never ring again with the revving of engines and the hammer of steel.

The garage may be idle, but the wind's been busy. Each corner of the yard has its own pile of litter, like it's having a competition: fizzy drinks bottles and plastic bags, crisp bags and burger boxes, sweet wrappers, ciggy packets, manky milk cartons . . .

A car! turning into the street. A taxi. Couldn't be.

Could it?

The taxi pulls up. Out steps Fifi, smart trousers, white shirt, cool and clean. Puts down his case in the road and pays his fare, like a man in a movie going to meet his girl. The taxi U-turns away.

'Hopper, how are you, my friend?'

'I thought you wasn't coming.'

'I'm sorry I'm late.'

'I was sure you wasn't coming.'

'*Ji wuahumi*, relax, dry your tears, old chap . . .' He takes out a hanky and pokes me face. '*Si abotre*, take it easy, everything's fine. It's just that a black man standing around after what happened this morning – not a good idea. Taxi looks more legal, don't you think? So, this is it?'

I take him inside, wind up the shutters. The place smells damp and swims with dust like those Christmas roundy things you shake to get the snow going. He looks round and goes, *Hmmm*. He's seen bigger and better. I show him the office, with its prints of MGs and Triumphs from the sixties, grimy filing cabinets and the old desk.

I lift the phone, wait for a ringing sound. 'It's working! You can call Africa.'

He smiles a funny smile. Maybe he's no-one left at home to call.

'This office was black with people once,' says I, '– if you know what I mean. Customers, secretaries, mechanics – Formula One drivers! Famous jockeys! Football stars! Look!'

I point out a framed photo of Micky Martin, who skippered Ballybriggan Wanderers when me da was in nappies, with his arms round me grandad after having his Bubble Car re-sprayed red and white.

I show Fifi the little kitcheny bit where you can boil a kettle and wash cups, and the door marked CONFESSIONAL which looks like a cupboard but is really the jacks.

'This is great,' he says. 'You must be proud of your daddy.'

'We'll have to get you a bed,' says I. 'I'll talk to me uncle. He'd do anything for anyone.'

What am I saying? Uncle Maddy wouldn't give Fifi the spit off his beer.

'Don't worry about me. After gardening all day, I sleep upside down like a bat.'

He sits down at the desk, setting off a little cloud of dust. He's gone quiet. Something's troubling him. How do I ask what I'm dying to ask?

'Why did you bring me here?'

'Why did I . . . ? To get you out of the rain.'

'What else?'

I meet his eyes and look down. And up again. His eyes are serious.

'Can you save me da's garage?'

My question floats in the dust like a sub waiting to be blown out the water. He looks at me. He's angry. He's mad. He's going to shout at me, tell me to get out and not be so cheeky.

A smile's coming up, crinkling his face. He's not mad, he's not going to shout. 'I thought so.

Only problem, I work five days for Mrs Quincy.'

'Do you have to? Can't you do four – or three – or one or two?'

Please, Fifi, be my African fairy godmother!

'It's a big garden, Hopper, and she's a nice lady and she's been good to me and pays well, and she's not supposed to. Still . . .' He sighs.

'Still what?'

Me heart fizzes with hope. If he says no, I think I'll be sick.

He leans back gazing at the ceiling, hands behind his head, like a company boss considering a dicey move.

'I nearly have the garden under control . . .' he says, humming to himself as he thinks, his velvety voice sanding the walls.

'I suppose I could cut my hours . . . but, Hopper, listen,' he goes, sitting up, eyes wide, 'I can fix most cars, but I can't do the books too, answer the phone, order the parts, go to the bank and so on. And you'd need publicity. This is not a job for one.'

'I got it all worked out, Fifi! Me cousins! Geri May's only thirteen, but she's got a computer and would make a great secretary. And Peach is a whiz with figures and does accounts. And um, let me see – Ambrose doesn't say much, but he loves cars and is brilliant at jigsaw puzzles. And I'll help. I could do publicity! No worries, Fifi, the cars will be back like wasps to jam! What d'you say?'

110

'I say you're a bright boy – but one small thing.'

'Money. You're worried about the money. I'll start paying soon as it starts flowing, honest!'

'It's not that. Your cousins, have you spoken to them?'

'Um – not yet. I got to be careful. Cousin Peach is a bit, well – prickly, you know?'

'Like how, prickly?'

'Um, he and me uncle don't exactly like my da.'

'They don't like your father?'

'Family feud.'

'That's not a good start, Hopper. What else?'

'They're not crazy about foreigners and refugees either. Apart from that, they're real nice – and me auntie's on your side already.'

'So you're saying we have a secretary of thirteen, an accountant who hates me already, and a boy who does puzzles,' says Fifi, keeping a straight face.

'You want to see the workshop, Fifi? It's real modern!'

What am I saying? It's real basic, not like Da's rivals with their fancy equipment.

'Except the overalls,' I remember. 'I was supposed to get them cleaned.'

'No thanks,' he says. 'Not now.' He gets up and looks out the window, across the yard that used to be backed up with all kinds of cars, but lies wasted now.

111

'Are you thinking about it, Fifi?'

'Yes.'

'Will it take long?'

'It will if you keep interrupting.'

'It's just that Auntie Gracie will be looking at the clock. I'm never usually this late. She'll call the cops, and they'll call Interpol, and they'll put out an intergalactic alert . . . No, wait. Relax – *ji wuahumi*, Rooney! They're at an auction, so we're OK.'

'Can you swim, Hopper?'

'A bit, why?'

'You're getting into deep water.'

'Me dad's sick and desperate, that's deep enough. Just think if I could go in and say, *Da, you'll never guess, Rooney's Motor Repairs is up and running again!*'

He takes a big sigh, like he's thinking about all the antelopes dying of drought and elephants shot by poachers he wishes he could save.

'D'you get snakes in Ghana? I love snakes.'

'Of course.'

'Do they bite?'

'Not if you leave them alone.'

'Do you get vipers in your garden?'

'Occasionally.'

'What else?'

'You might find a *nanka* in a drainpipe.'

'Dangerous?'

'They can kill. You need a particular stone to

112

lay on the bite to draw the poison. Bind the wound above the bite to stop the venom spreading, and use herbs to – what's the word? – fight the poison.'

'And cobras?'

'They try and steal my aunt's eggs.'

'How does she stop them?'

'Place three eggs together in the coop. The middle one you've cooked. When it eats the cooked egg, it gets ill and slow and easy to catch.'

'Doesn't it attack?'

'If you upset it, it spits in your eye, blinding you for a moment, and then it strikes!' *Pshoo!* he demonstrates, slapping me arm and making me jump.

'I wish I had a cobra for Peach and Uncle Maddy. I hate them. Sometimes I want to run away.'

'What would that serve?'

'Auntie keeps a little stash of notes in a tea tin. I could catch a train to Galway and catch fish.'

'And who looks after this place, while you're fishing in Galway?'

I can't look at him. If he says no, I'll cry. I've not cried in a while, but the floodwaters are rising and this time, I'll flood the garage, the street, the whole of Ballybriggan, taking Peach and Uncle Maddy with me, out to sea on a river of muck.

'How did you get the scar under your eye?'

'When I was a baby. They cut me. It's the mark of my people.'

'Does it tell other people who you are?'

'Yes.'

'Like a football scarf you can never take off.'

'If you like.'

'Handy for friends, not so good if you run into enemies?'

He nods slowly, and I'm starting to get a feeling of what happened to him at home.

'Did you support the wrong team, Fifi?'

'I'm sorry?'

I'm looking at him, his scar and his hands and calm sad eyes.

'Fifi?' Here goes, one last try. 'I need your help. Nothing else makes sense. This holiday's going to end soon, and I'll be back in school playing the eejit and trying not to think of Da fading away in hospital and Mam living it up in London. You're all the hope I got.'

His eyes are clear and cool gazing out at the breeze kicking litter round the yard. This is it. His mind's working fast. It's in his eyes, like an arrow from a crossbow flying to its target.

Split the apple on the boy's head – or kill the boy, stone dead.

'I'll have to talk to Ellen.'

'Who?'

'Mrs Quincy.'

Whisper, 'Yeah, sure.'

'Reassure her I'll find time for the garden.'

'Right.'

'I wouldn't wish to let her down.'

'No.'

Another big sigh . . . more zebras and wildebeest to save.

'It's a very big challenge.'

'Very big.'

'I can't promise anything . . .'

He's stopped speaking, he's just gazing, picturing how he's going to do it – or how he's going to get out of it, and this time when I go to speak, I'm so dry not even a whisper comes out. Waggling me tongue and swallowing, trying to drag me voice out of me throat so I can try begging – when he gets up out the chair and lays a hand on me shoulder, like an eagle, softly, to save me or tear me to bits.

'All right, my friend, I'll try, I'll do my best.'

Teasing Mr Crocodile

When I get back, everyone's still out and the house is quiet.

Soon change that.

'Yes! YES! *Y-E-S-S-S-S-S-S!*' I yell in and out the kitchen, and up and down the stairs. 'Roll up, ye racy Renaults! Ye sappy Citroëns and poxy Porsches!' Fifi said yes, and I could scream! I could fly, I could eat the carpet! 'Volvos and custard! Toyotas on toast! Fifi said YES! He'll do his best!' I'm so jizzed up I could—

Holy Spooks! It's Scary Mary again, in the doorway, looking at me like she's caught me dancing in me noony.

'Don't worry, Geri May, I've not gone mad.'

'You're mad already,' she goes, 'and don't forget our deal. I never went out and you never thieved, right? Cos if ever you grass me up, I'll delete you and send you to the recycling bin for ever!'

'Wait! Come back, Fifi said yes!'

She's gone up to her room and closed the door. She's in one of her strops and now's probably not the moment, but I got to talk to her. If she doesn't say yes, the whole thing's over before it's begun. I can hear her upstairs listening to Wet Life or Boys Home or some other poncy boy band.

Here we go, carefully up the stairs to stand outside her door. She's singing along to her music.

Knock and go in.

'Hey! Who said come in?'

'It's real important, Geri May.'

'It better be.'

She's at her computer. I approach all interested.

'They look cool, who are they?'

The band she's playing is up on screen, handsome yobs with fascinating lives. *Brett is really easy-going, loves parties and gets invited to lots, as you can imagine.*

'Stop being so nosy. What d'you want?'

'How would you like to be in my show? *Rooney's Motor Repairs Rides Again*, starring Hopper and Fifi, and the very—' *Whoops!* Nearly said 'lovely' Geri May!

'You're melting me brain, Hopper Rooney.'

'I'm serious. I'm looking for a secretary for the garage.'

'What garage?'

'Me da's, silly.'

117

'Don't get smart, Sparrowfart!'

'I'm not messing, Geri May, Fifi said yes!'

'Give us a break, Hopper! Me da's a rat, Peach's a pig and Ambo's a disaster on legs—'

'You're not listening.'

'And then you have to come along and wreck me head. I'm going crazy I'm so bored!'

'It wouldn't be boring running the office.'

'And I hate the lot of youse, me mam and all, for letting him ground me.'

'WILL YOU JUST LISTEN FOR A MINUTE!'

Geri May looks at me amazed.

'Doesn't anybody listen in this house?' says I. 'God wasted five pairs of ears on you lot!'

'Who are you to criticize my family?' she goes.

'At least I got one.'

I can't believe she said that, and said it with a twisty smile I'd like to rub out with sandpaper. My turn to walk out and slam the door. Stomp to me room and slam that one too.

Alone in me room – Ambo's room, not mine – I open a drawer, remove a jumper and a blanket of tissue and sneak a look at me selection of warriors and siege weapons.

Footsteps on the landing. The door opens, enter Geri May.

'Did anyone say come in?' says I.

'Don't get all steamed up over nothing.'

'Over nothing?'

'Don't you ever say things you don't mean?'

I can't look at her. She's right. I've no family. Mam's gone and never coming back. Da's in hospital and never coming out.

'You're right, nobody listens,' she says. 'I been asking Ma for weeks to sew me jeans, and each time I remind her, she goes, "What jeans?"'

'Can't you sew your own jeans?'

'I don't do sewing. What you got there?' Geri May moves in close to look at me most private possessions. I turn to ice. If she laughs or says something horrible . . . She picks up an Arctic Bowman, and then a Valhallan Bodyguard, and turns them over in her hands. 'I better go and wash off this nail polish before me da gets back and kills me,' she says, putting back me treasures like they're any old thing. Then she turns at the door and says, 'What d'you want a secretary for anyway?'

'Fifi's willing to try and get me da's garage going again, but we need you in the office and someone else to do the accounts.'

She folds her arms, screws up her eyes. 'If you're spoofing me . . .'

'I'm not spoofing, I'm sick of spoofing. Don't you understand, me da's going to die if I don't save his garage?'

'Mmm,' she goes. 'I'll have to talk to me agent.'

With that she walks out.

And walks back in again. 'And what will you be doing?'

Shrugging. 'I used to hang around me da, but never paid much attention. I'm just an eejit, everyone knows that. Maybe I'll just sit behind the desk smoking a big cigar.'

Geri May laughs – I made her laugh!

'So who's doing the accounts, Mr cigar-smoking boss?'

'Peach.'

'*Peach?* Accounts for your da's garage?'

'Why not?'

'Don't you know about your da and mine?'

'It's nothing to do with Peach.'

'Yeah, but Peach is Da's lap-dog!' She laughs real bitter and walks off going, 'Sit boy, heel boy, have a biscuit!'

I go after her. She stands holding her door, not letting me in.

'Listen, Hip-hop, I can't get Peach to pass the butter, so how are you going to get him to help your da?'

'I'll talk to him.'

'Don't make me laugh!'

'He's got to say yes.'

'You get Peach Rooney to say yes, and I'll quit school and be a nun.'

'But what about you, Geri May? You haven't said yes, or no.'

'I don't know nothing about being a secretary.'

120

'You'd soon learn.'

'What would I have to do?'

'Answer the phone, order parts, make out bills – you're good at sums. We could use your computer and printer.'

'Is that it?'

'You'd need to wear respectable clothes and get up real early.'

'You got a nerve, Hopper Rooney.'

Bang! goes her door.

Was that a yes?

I lie awake, imagining Geri May as a nun, me mind a hive of worries. How's Fifi spending his first lonely night in the garage, and which way's Geri May going to jump, and what are the chances of Peach going against his own da and saying yes for mine?

It's hopeless – hopeless – hopeless.

Out in the night a knackered Civil War tank coming up the street – Uncle's limping Volvo. In swans Auntie and Uncle all squiffy and gargled and going *Shhhh!* as Auntie bangs around in the kitchen and Uncle clatters up the stairs and into me room carrying Ambo's dead weight and tucks him into bed whispering, 'Sleep well, my little pumpkin head.'

The night keeps going. Geri May will say NO! tomorrow, Peach will laugh in me face and in any case, the cops have probably raided the garage and dragged Fifi off.

Ambo snores like a chainsaw, and here comes a motorbike tearing up the road, smacking the gate open. Peach in a mood, kicking around downstairs and playing the TV too loud, till Uncle roars down the stairs to lower it for Jeez' sake, waking half the neighbourhood himself.

Then it all goes quiet, just the faintest hum of Peach on his mobile somewhere below, pleading for his life.

Then there's squeaking on the landing, not a thief or a ghost, Geri May putting her head in me door and whispering, 'You awake, Hop?'

'Yep.'

'She ditched him.'

'Who?'

'Peach's girl ditched him! Tried talking her round but it didn't work. He's always ditching them. Taste of his own medicine. Don't go near him tomorrow.'

I hear Peach dragging himself up to bed like a corpse.

I wait all morning for Peach to get up. When he does, it's not the sorry cousin who crawled to bed with a hole in his heart – it's a maddened bull! Throwing himself around in the shower, banging pots in the kitchen.

You'd be mad to ask him now, I tell meself, and I agree, but can't help it. Patience isn't me best event. I'm like the feller on his knees training to be a priest who goes, 'Lord, teach me patience – but hurry, will ye!'

'Peach?' Follow him up to his room. 'Peach, can I ask you something?'

He's not avoiding me. He's just red with rage and black with sorrow and I'm an insect. I knock and go in.

He's not looking so good, sprawled on the bed, eyes blotchy, face the colour of mustard. The room pongs of strawberries and aftershave.

'Peach . . . ?'

His mobile goes. While he's talking DJ business, I go over to his aquarium and gaze through ferny plants at all the pretty fishies I'm getting to know, like the silvery scissortails and the beautiful blue and white zebra fish and the orange clouds of pygmy fish and the mini-shark with its red-hot tail, and the lonely Siamese fighting fish which can't share with another male cos he'll go for it – he'll even attack his own reflection in a mirror.

Peach comes off the phone, reaches in the fruit bowl and falls back on the bed.

'What d'you want, kid – can't you see I'm dying?'

'I'm real sorry about your girl.'

'What!' Mad! 'Who told you that?'

'It's in all the papers and on telly – Peach *The Hunk* Rooney breaks up with Miss World.'

'Miss World!' he laughs, crunching into kiwi,

skin and all. 'Miss Nose-in-the-air, more like. Who needs them anyway?'

'Does that mean you'll have a bit more free time?'

'What are you angling at?'

'Want me to get you something for your head?'

'Don't ever drink, Hopper. You may as well stick pins in your brain. If you do drink, fruit's the business for hangovers . . .' He groans, stretching for strawberries.

'Peach, can I ask a flavour – I mean, favour?'

'Puts juice back in the brain and sweetens the blood.'

'Would you help in me da's garage?'

'Restores the vitamin C the booze butchers.'

'And do the accounts?'

'And steer clear of girls, Hop-scotch. They lull you with kisses and cut you to ribbons.'

'And go to the bank?'

''Course, with your looks, Hops, you won't have too many girls to worry about. What bank? What are you on about?'

That wasn't very nice and I feel like dunking his head in the aquarium, letting the Siamese fighting fish loose on his tongue.

'I want you to do me da's accounts,' says I, hot and angry.

A cruel look comes over his face. 'What did you say?'

'My friend Fifi from Ghana's getting the garage going, and I was wondering—'

He's sitting up slow and mean. It's possible he's going to kill me. I can see the headstone – MICHAEL HOPPER ROONEY MURDERED BY COUSIN PEACH WHILE MUNCHING A KIWI – R.I.P. Except people would go, *Which one was munching the kiwi?*

'Did you say accounts? For your da's garage?' Peach swings his legs off the bed and faces me, eyes like broken glass. 'Do you know what you're saying – or are you the biggest eejit that ever breathed?'

'Me da's wittling away in hospital, and if I'm an eejit for wanting to help him . . .'

'Don't you know your da stabbed mine in the back? Kicked his elder brother in the gutter.'

'He's too young for all this,' says Geri May popping up in the doorway – *again!*

Peach lashes a finger at her. 'Keep out of it, toe rag!'

'Make me, sleazebag!'

'Stop it, please,' says I, as Peach starts wrestling Geri May out the room.

'Just cos you got a sick head,' Geri May fights back, 'no need to dump on Hopper.'

'Please don't fight, I need help,' says I talking to meself as usual.

'Mind your own business, witch!' says Peach, tipping Geri May onto the landing.

'It's family business, and I'm family in case you hadn't noticed!' goes Geri May, shaking him off and marching back in again.

The row brings Ambo in. Peach tries shutting him out, but Ambo wriggles free and tumbles in laughing.

'Are youse all off your heads?' goes Peach. 'If Ma and Da got wind of this – Jeez, what's the time? Where is she anyway? Is Da coming home for lunch?'

'Cool it, Peach. Ma's got to know,' says Geri May. 'We're not keeping it from her.'

Peach can't believe what he's hearing and has to sit down. 'Peel me an orange, quick, Hopper,' he says. 'This is serious.'

'Does that mean you'll consider it,' says I, opening an orange. He pinches off a piece and closes his eyes to let the juices run down his throat.

'We're dead monkeys if Da finds out.'

'Map!' goes Ambo, clapping his arms together on the floor. 'Map-map!'

'Not now, Ambo, can't you see I'm thinking?'

'Does that mean you're considering it?' says I again.

'It means you're all crazy.'

'Map-map!'

'Drop it, Ambo!'

'But you said monkeys,' Geri May laughs.

'What's that got to do with it?'

'Anyone says monkeys and he goes—'

'Map-map!'

'Why does he go *MAP* when I go monkeys, for Jeez' sakes?'

'Map means snap!' Geri May in stitches. 'Three little monkeys sitting in a tree, teasing Mr Crocodile – *you can't catch me! you can't catch me!* – but along comes the crocodile quiet as can be and—'

'Map-map!' goes Ambo, delighted with himself.

Peach rubs his sore head and paces the room. 'And just what exactly does your African know about garages?'

'He's a mechanic! Worked in garages from Bindalu to Timbuktu. And guess what? Geri May's thinking about running the office.'

'What!'

'Why not?' goes Geri May.

'You're only a kid. What do you know about running an office?'

'What d'you think we learn in school, ye big thick?'

'She's the bee's knees with PCs,' says I, 'and I'll have a crack at publicity and chatting up old customers – if you don't mind doing accounts and all the rest.'

'What's the rest? Shining her shoes?'

'Yeah, and flapping your ears when me fan packs in!' goes Geri May.

'And buy in ice-creams when it's hot,' says I panicking, 'and get Richard Gere a beer when he rolls up in his Roller . . .'

'Cop on, Peach,' goes Geri May, 'this is an emergency.'

'You saying you'll do it, Geri May?' I cry out.

'Maybe.'

'Maybe?'

'Let's get this straight,' goes Peach. 'The African's the tools, Geri May's the brains, Hopper's the hype – what have you got for me, apart from accounts?'

'Security,' says I.

'Security?'

'Riding shotgun to the bank, stepping in when customers get snotty and leaning on the gate looking hard.'

'Mmm,' goes Peach. 'And what would I wear?'

'Your bike gear,' says Geri May. 'Look at all them goons minding every door in town. Black leather and a face like a fridge. Shouldn't be too hard.'

'Except I work full-time.'

'You're always saying they owe you holidays.'

Peach breathes deep and looks out the window. 'You're all crazy.'

'I know, Peach,' says I, 'but will you do it?'

'You got some nerve, Hopper Rooney . . . some nerve.'

I look down, gutted. Without a half-decent

accountant, we're— Ouch! Somebody's pinching me. It's Geri May, telling me to keep at him. 'There might be some money,' says I, not knowing what I'm saying, 'and kickbacks and sidekicks and—'

'Who gives a monkey's about money?' says Peach. 'It's me da we got to—'

'Map-map!' goes Ambo, slapping his arms together. 'Map-map!'

'Maybe it's time we stood up to him,' says Geri May.

'To who?'

'Da!'

'You nuts?'

'He's thrown his weight around long enough.'

'Da's the rock of this family, and I'm sticking with him.'

'Da's the bully of this family, and I'm sick of him.'

'You're a disgrace to this family, Geri May. They should have drowned you at birth.'

Geri May goes white. She can dish it, but she can't take it, and she's yelling things you never hear in our house, and he's laughing at her.

'THAT'S IT! If youse two won't help, I'll find someone else,' says I storming out – or starting to, when Peach flings out a hairy arm and spins me round again.

'Cool off, cousin! We're airing views, OK? This is too serious to jump into blind. Making your da happy could turn mine into a serial killer. Is that what you want?'

Ambo's making new noises. 'Bow-wow-we . . . bow-wow-we?'

'Zip it, Ambo! That's enough!'

'Bow-wow-we?'

'Cut it out!'

Geri May's laughing again. 'What about me? he's saying. Don't want to miss the fun, eh, Ambo? All we got to do is find you a job.'

He looks at us, wise as a wall.

'Good man yourself,' says Peach, 'but how the heck could you help?'

'He could help me post flyers!' says I.

'And carry a sandwich board,' says Geri May.

'What's a sandwich board?' says I.

'One of them yokes you wear round your neck saying *Jesus Loves You*, or in this case *Rooney's Motor Repairs Loves You!*'

Peach disgusted, 'I'm not having our kid carrying no sandwich board.'

'You rather him rot at home?'

Peach looks me in the eye. 'So you know about the bad blood between your da and ours?'

Me, nodding, 'Grandad left the garage to your da and mine, on condition your da stop gambling. But he broke the deal, blew all the loot. My da told him to get lost, and it's been icebergs ever since.'

'Your da never gave ours a chance,' Peach snarls at me. 'Just slung him out. He was going to pay it all back, but your da wanted to take him to court!'

'Why can't we just forget all that!' goes Geri May.

'Da-da-da,' goes Ambo.

'Forget it?' explodes Peach. 'It was like a murder in the family!'

'Da-da-da!'

'He's heard a car,' says Geri May, 'and it's not any old car.'

'Stay cool, everyone,' goes Peach, panicking. 'Not a word. This conversation never happened!'

'But it did happen, Peach!' I yell. 'And I need to know if you two are with me, and I need to know now!'

Peach looks at Geri May, Geri May looks at Peach.

Downstairs Uncle Maddy comes in singing. Good day at the office.

The rain's back, lashing the windows and leaping the gutters. I lie awake thinking, Thank God Fifi's got a roof. I drift away and dream about him hanging upside down from a beam in our school hall, and Mrs Scully – me new teacher! – flying round going, *Saints preserve us, we're infested with bats! Call Pest Control! Call the Guards!*

Cool it, miss, I'm saying, *it's only my friend Fifi having a nap . . .*

Knock! Knock!

Who's there?

Someone's knocking on the wall. The same someone is creeping in the door going, 'You awake, Hopper?'

Downstairs you can hear the TV on and Uncle Maddy's wheezy voice and Auntie's smoky replies.

Geri May sits on me bed in the dark in her jim-jams, and I can barely speak for the bubbles in me heart.

'I been thinking,' she whispers, 'about being secretary. And it's bad news.'

No! I can't take it.

'I'll do it.'

'What?'

'But only if Peach says yes too.'

'Why's that bad news?'

'Getting killed by your own da?'

'We'll keep it secret.'

'I wish! Shhh, listen!'

A rusty engine coming up the street like a swarm of bees. Peach!

When he gets in, he says goodnight to his ma and da and comes straight up. We're hiding in the shadows on the landing.

'*Huh!*' he breathes. 'You trying to scare me to death!'

Geri May grabs him. 'Have you thought about – you know?'

'*Shhh!* 'Course, what else? Me head's wrecked with it. Got all me music mixed up – slow when they wanted to dance, dance when they wanted it slow.'

'Did you decide?' I whisper, hopping up and down with hope.

'Yes – and no,' he answers, hopping up and down cos he's dying for a pee. 'I'm in if Geri's in – and as long as Ma says it's OK, and he doesn't find out,' he says pointing downstairs.

'You m-mean it?'

'But I'm not taking orders from no African.'

'I could hug you, Peach.'

'Don't! Now get to bed, the pair of youse!'

'Peach?'

'*What?*'

'You don't hate me da?'

'I don't know him. I was a kid.'

'Peach?'

'*What?*'

'It could be a good crack.'

'Yeah, that's what I was thinking,' he says, and dives into the jacks.

I'm looking at Geri May looking at me in the dark. I smile at her and she smiles back.

'So, when are you leaving school?' I whisper.

'What?'

'Or have you forgot – *Sister*?'

Hopper the Copper

Next morning, Peach drags himself off to work, and I shake Ambo awake going, 'Rise and shine, cousin! All we got to do is ask your ma, and you and me will be working for my da! What d'you say to that?'

Uncle Maddy's gone to work. I got to catch Auntie before she cycles over to join him. But first we got to wake Geri May.

'Come on, Geri May, wake up!'

Groans, more groans and nothing doing. Getting Geri May out of bed's like pulling a bad tooth.

'Is this how you're planning to run the office – from inside your duvet?' says I, and run down to the kitchen where bacon's frying with the radio on.

'Auntie, guess what? I'm so happy!'

'Who's happy, pet?'

'*The overturned truck on the Malahide Road's been cleared, but they're still – can you believe it! – rounding up chickens.*'

'The garage, Auntie – it's going ahead!'

'The garage is what, pet?'

'*So continue to avoid the area – unless you don't mind fresh-laid eggs on your car roof.*'

'Fifi said yes if me cousins say yes, and Geri May said yes if Peach says yes, and he said yes if she says yes and you say yes—'

'That's a lot of yesses for this time of the morning, pet.'

'*And that burst water main in Dolphin's Barn has turned the area into a lake, so . . .*'

'But you won't tell Uncle, Auntie – cos we don't want blood on the carpet, do we?'

'They could do with a clean anyway, pet.'

'*If you fancy a paddle on your way to work, head for Dolphin's Barn—*'

Whoops! What have I done? Gone and switched off the radio!

Auntie's looking puzzled. 'Not another one?' she goes, trying a light, which works, of course.

'Sorry, Auntie, I must have turned it off.'

'That's all right, pet. Pop it on again.'

'Before I do, Auntie, is it OK if Ambrose helps advertise the garage – if I can get him out of bed?'

'Not again!' she goes.

'What?'

'He's not done it for ages.'

'No, Auntie, he's not wet the bed . . .'

'Thanks be to Jesus.'

135

I give up. Getting through to Auntie's like opening a can with your teeth. Leave it to Geri May.

Jump on me bike and go looking for Fifi. I've got this sickening feeling I got to see him, hear him say once more that he's going to do it, make sure he's not changed his mind. One small problem – how to find him? He said Mrs Quincy lives in Chapelizod, something about a view over the river to the park, and walking her to her hubby's grave.

Pedal hard to Chapelizod and the only cemetery in sight, and start looking for big houses that see over the river to the park. Try one – no Mrs Ellen Quincy, only a terrier sniffing me uncles – I mean ankles. Try another – no Mrs Quincy, only an old grouch going, 'Private property – can't you read?' Try a third house, and this time there's a beautiful old lady in the garden, sitting under a brolly playing chess with nobody.

'Hello there!' she waves, jingling bracelets. 'May I help you?'

'Are you Mrs Quincy? And do you know where Fifi is?'

'Ah, you must be Topper!'

'Hopper.'

'The young chap who wants to steal my Fifi away.'

'I'm sorry, missus—'

'No need. Your poor father. Pour yourself some lemonade, Topper, throw your eye over this game and tell me how to beat Fifi before he gets back from massacring my poor flowers!'

'But I don't know chess, missus.'

'What? Don't they teach you anything in school these days?'

Here comes Fifi, secateurs in hand and a big grin.

'Look who it is! The boy detective.'

'That's me, Detective Sergeant Inspector Hopper.'

'Fifi, how on earth's this poor boy going to get on in life if he can't play chess?'

'Only one thing for it, Mrs Quincy . . .'

'We'll have to teach him!'

Well, isn't this the life! Sitting in the shade playing chess and sipping lemonade Mrs Quincy made herself with real lemons and real ade, chatting about this-an'-that and me da's garage – and guess what? Mrs Quincy's loaning Fifi a camp bed, pillows and tea-towels, her late hubby's bathrobe, a duvet and spare toaster. It's all looking good, and I'm all relaxed and tingly – until her son Rick drives up and spoils it all like a brick in the head.

'Why is it every time I drop by, he's sitting doing nothing?' says Rick the Brick without even looking at Fifi, who stands up smiling real polite.

Rick's a flashy feller gone to seed. Too much nosh and no physical. Puffy cheeks and a bouncy belly.

'Pour yourself some iced lemonade, Rickie dear,' says Mrs Quincy, 'over your head, if possible.'

'No need for that, Mother. I'm only thinking of you.'

'Shall I return to my work?' says Fifi.

'Good heavens, no. Stay right where you are!'

'It's not a laughing matter, Mother. This scoundrel has you wrapped round his finger. Asylum seeker indeed. Gentleman of leisure, more like.'

'Really? Have you noticed the garden lately? It's never been more beautiful.'

'Funny, I thought gardens were God's work.' Rick taking the mick.

'Yes, but God can't wield the hoe and work the hose Himself. Fifi is His handmaiden, and I consider myself blessed.'

'*Hmmph!*' goes Rick, sweating buckets after his strenuous hike from the car. Pours a glass and sees me. 'Who's this? The Artful Dodger?'

'Topper, dear, meet my charming son Rickie, who, as you can see, is entirely without sin. Fifi's helping Topper rescue his ailing father's garage. A noble enterprise, if ever there was one.'

'You can bring us your car!' says I to Sticky Rickie.

138

'I beg your pardon?'

'We'll give you a good deal.'

'Most kind,' goes Rick, his face saying, *You really think I'd bring my precious car to your grubby garage?*

Shocking Auntie

This is the last hurdle. It's nine in the evening, we're all lounging watching the news – high-life sleaze, street crime, crashes, floods and missing teenagers, a bundle of laughs – waiting for Uncle to go so we can get Auntie alone.

'Why's everyone so quiet?' notices Uncle Maddy. 'You're usually noisy as a monkey-house.'

'Map-map!' goes a voice under the table.

Uncle goes and showers, puts on a tasselly shirt and boots, grabs the guitar he keeps stuck together with tape and heads out singing a soppy song he'll be belting out for his fans in Kelly's Bar.

'No matter how mean you treat me,
You'll always be my Sweetpea.
Your kisses are cruel,
But they'll always rule
My heart . . .'

140

Listening to him drive away, we all go *ffffff* like we been holding our breaths under water.

'So what's this you're all scheming?' says Auntie. 'Must be something weird and wonderful if you're all talking to each other.'

Peach nudges Geri May, she nudges me, and I've no-one to nudge, so it's me to ruin Auntie's evening.

'It's about me da's garage, Auntie.'

The weatherman's smiling. Sunny to start, rain sweeping in from the west. Peach grabs the zapper and zaps him. Auntie's shocked. She never misses the weather. Peach is pointing at me.

'We're getting me da's garage going, Auntie. Fifi the mechanic, Geri May the office, Peach the books and me and Ambo the hard sell. What d'you think of . . . ?'

The blood drains from her face. She stares at us in turn. 'If Maddy hears you even discussed this . . .'

No-one dares breathe. I hear meself swallow – *gulp*.

Auntie to Geri May, 'You're supposed to be grounded.'

'I'll start early and get home early.'

To Peach, 'And you're working.'

'I'm taking holidays from next week. Two weeks I'm owed.'

Shocked, 'You're not seriously thinking of involving Ambrose?'

Ambo looks up from his game of spin the spoon under our feet.

'How's he going to make progress, Ma,' says Geri May, 'if he spends his life under the table?'

Auntie takes her hand away from her mouth and lets out the longest sigh since Creation.

'I can understand Geri May getting back at her da, but you, son?'

'I dunno, Ma,' says Peach, hands in pockets and talking to his feet. 'Maybe I'm tired of this family war, tired of Da telling us who we can and can't talk to. It's not nice for Hopper. Not nice for any of us.'

'You wouldn't say that to your father's face.'

'No, Ma, I enjoy living.'

'Face it, Ma, he's a bully,' says Geri May.

'Your father feels things deep, and I won't have you disrespecting him. And another thing. I take it you've spoken to your father, Hopper?'

'I've not seen him, Auntie.'

'I hope you weren't thinking of acting without his blessing?'

'You think we can do it then, Ma?' says Geri May.

'Not a hope. What you're taking on is much too big. But just trying is success enough and I applaud you all. Go see your da, Hopper – Geri May can go with you. And another thing, I want to meet this Fifi.'

Peach's chin nearly dislocates itself. 'But Ma, he's . . .'

'What! A Hell's Angel? An Eskimo? A Martian? If he's going to be working for Eddie, someone's got to check him out. Invite him for coffee. In the meantime, I don't like all this going on behind Maddy's back.'

'But Mam!' goes Geri May and Peach together.

'I'll give you three weeks. By then you're all back in school or work, and this whole idea will have fallen on its face, and Maddy need never know. If, however, by some miracle you get the garage going, you'll have to own up to your father.'

'That's terrific!' laughs Geri May. 'Fail, and we live. Succeed and we fry.'

Peach, 'I think I'm gonna call the undertaker.'

Geri May, 'I think I'm gonna throw up.'

While Peach and Geri May plan their funerals, I call the garage. The phone rings and rings – Fifi's taken ill, he's gone home, he's dead!

'Hello?'

'Fifi! It's me! They said yes! We'll be over in the morning. What time you want us?'

'Don't rush. Say about eight?'

'How's eight in the morning?' I yell.

Peach and Geri May's faces go, *You got to be joking!*

'Sounds fine, Fifi!'

Storm in a Peppermint Tea Cup

7 a.m. Ambo's up as always, stretched out on the deck squinting at a jigsaw he's planning to attack.

Stick me head out the door. Uncle Maddy's snoring for Ireland.

Tip-toe in to Peach – he's awake too, measuring up in the mirror, preparing to meet the African.

Tip-toe in to wake Geri May, but for her it's the middle of the night.

'Geri May, it's me. Please wake up.'

Even in death she looks lovely, and I'm thinking of the dishy prince hacking a way in with a machete to wake Sleeping Beauty with a kiss. It's tempting.

'Come on, Geri May, the big day – remember?'

'Huh? Wozza time?'

'It's after seven, come on, we're meeting Fifi!'

'Leave uzz alone.'

I try tugging a limp arm.

'Go away.'

A stray foot.

'Leave off!' she lashes out.

Jumping back, 'Jesus, Mary and Joseph, Geri May! Waking you's like pulling a pit bull off a kid's leg.'

Try tugging arm *and* foot.

'Get away, you freak of nature!' she goes.

Me eyes sting. That wasn't very nice.

Run whispering to Peach, 'You got to help, she won't get up.'

Both run in to Geri May – the ghost is sitting up! Green eyes flickering dangerously.

'Give us two secs,' she says.

Minutes later, we're all sneaking down to grab a bite of breakfast.

A door creaks above— Hearts freeze. It's Uncle Maddy, shotgun in hand, fixing to blow us to Hell in a hail of bullets.

Phew! It's only Auntie tip-toeing down to lend Geri May her bike.

Hysterical whispers. 'Bye, Ma!' – 'Bye, Auntie!' – 'Good luck!' – and we're away, Ambo squashed inside a spare helmet clinging to Peach on his shrieking Yamaha, and me and Geri May pedalling like eejits to keep up.

We lose them half-way through Donnyglas and take a breather.

'I'm done in,' she chokes, 'and I don't even smoke.'

I'm not speaking to her after what she called me earlier, and anyway I'm too worried. What if me cousins hate Fifi? What if Da doesn't want us to save his garage? What if we do everything right and no customers show, and they find us dead at our posts oozing maggots?

We press on, legs beat and brains melting, and find Peach and Ambo hiding in the lane like hoods waiting to bust a corner shop. The gate to Rooney's Motor Repairs is wide open. 'You first,' goes Peach – 'Me?' – and off I go, proud as Punch, leading me army into Da's yard.

The wide slidy doors to the workshop are open, and there's Fifi to meet us, cool and handsome in his creamy jumpsuit.

Me heart lifts off. This is brilliant!

Fifi takes us into the office and pours five steaming cups of yellowy stuff. The mood is nervy. We all sit down except Peach – and Ambo, who's handcuffed to him with the toddler lead.

Peach pointing, 'What's that supposed to be?'

'Mint tea, fresh from my employer's garden.'

'I don't give a fig how fresh it is, I'm not drinking that. And another thing, I don't take no orders from foreigners or refugees.'

Holy hacksaws! This isn't what I planned.

'That's good, I like plain speaking,' says Fifi. 'Please sit down, I'll make you an everyday tea, and then let each person speak his mind.'

'Forget the tea!' goes Peach. 'Let's get on with it.' He sits and pulls Ambo onto a seat beside him.

'Will I introduce everyone?' says I all trembly.

'I can introduce meself,' says Peach, looking at Fifi. 'I'm Peter – Peach to me friends, Peter to you, till I say otherwise. I done loads of accounts, and I won't have no-one question me work.'

'Fine. I'm Kofi, Fifi to *my* friends. I'm a good mechanic and I work hard, and you were all twenty minutes late this morning.'

Peach stares at Fifi. Fifi kind of smiles back.

I can't stop shaking. Are we saving this garage, or burying it?

Fifi nods to Geri May. She blinks, and swallows. I've never seen her this edgy.

'I'm Geri May, and um – I'm only thirteen – and haven't a clue and wish I was home in bed.'

Peach laughs and claps his hands, and Fifi goes, 'That's OK, Geri May, we're all nervous. This is a mountain we're climbing. We need to support each other. What do you think, Peter?'

'I think the whole idea is crack-brained.'

147

'Then why you doing it, ye big thick?' goes Geri May.

Peach clams up, folds his arms.

Suddenly, lightning. Rumbles of thunder.

Fifi looks at Ambrose, who's been gazing at him with big eyes since he got here. 'You must be Ambrose. You're very welcome.'

'Who are you, welcoming everybody?' goes Peach. 'You're not the priest, you don't own the place.'

'Mind your manners, Peach!' goes Geri May.

'It's OK,' goes Fifi. 'Peter's right. I didn't mean to sound that way. Let's have no bosses here, only comrades.'

The sky's coming down, dark and heavy. Lightning whips the air, thunder clatters like hooves on the roofs.

'It's a warning!' says I. 'We got to bury our bygones and get along.'

Peach laughs. 'This is a joke.'

Geri May stares miserably.

Even Fifi looks lost, gazing home to Ghana.

Lightning floodlights the yard, thunder explodes overhead and soon the roofs and yard are running with rain and jumping with hailstones.

'Fay! Fay!' goes Ambo, tugging on his lead.

'Don't be afraid, Ambo,' says Geri May, 'it's only Himself doing his push-ups.'

'Your turn to introduce yourself, Ambrose,' says Fifi.

148

But Ambo buries his prickly head in Peach's lap.

'We should never have brung him,' says Peach.

'Hopper's turn,' says Fifi.

'Get on with it, kid,' says Peach, 'I got to get to work. This garage isn't everything.'

Wrong! I'm thinking. Da's in hospital, Mam's in England, school's round the corner, this is everything.

'Spit it out, Hopper, I got to go,' says Peach putting on his space helmet.

I'm on me feet, holding back the floods.

'Youse all got it wrong. There is a boss round here, and his name's Hopper, and that's me! And I'm saying this is everything, and anyone with better things to do can drop dead – I mean, drop out.' I feel the heat of Peach's eyes. I don't care. 'And if youse all want to fight, you can do it someplace else.'

Lightning rips the sky apart – wait for it, *bang!*

'Fay-fay!' wails Ambo in Peach's arms.

'It's OK, kid, it's moving on. Plenty more people to scare.'

'Please don't go yet, Peter,' says Fifi. 'We can't do this without you. You're – what's the word? Essential. You too, Geri May, and Hopper, and Ambrose – somehow I feel it already. We're a team.'

'Some team,' goes Peach.

149

'I've never answered phones before!' goes Geri May. 'Only a million times a day to me mates.'

'You'll be fine,' says Fifi. 'You got a nice voice, and I hear you're a computer expert.'

'You're joking me!' she says, red in the face. 'And it's no use, I'm grounded, I got to be in by five.'

'Then we'll work office hours around you, same as I need to work mine around Mrs Quincy.'

'And I've not done much publicity before,' says I. 'I've not done any!'

'No experience can be an advantage.'

'It can?'

'Sure. You come at things in your own fresh way.'

'To be honest,' Peach coughs inside his helmet, 'I've not done a lot of security, 'cept keeping me sister and brother in order.'

'You'll be fine,' says Fifi, 'the way you carry yourself with cool authority.'

Peach goes *hmm*, looks at his watch and lifts off his helmet. 'I suppose I could manage a few minutes. And I'll have that tea if it's still going, and make it strong.'

We get down to business – accounts and suppliers, prices and flyers and emergency measures for when Uncle Maddy finds out and comes after us with an axe.

And insurance. Very important. As Da

always says – *There's many a slip 'twixt cup and lip*.

The storm rolls away like a stone. Light blinds me eyes as I watch the others ride away home.

Fifi looks washed up.

'What's that, Fifi?' I'm looking at a disgusting mattress propped against a wall.

'I went walking last night and found it on a skip.'

'You didn't sleep on it, did you?'

I feel terrible. Fifi's doing all this for us, and he's sleeping on a pork pie sicked up by a dinosaur, with Da's manky overalls for sheets.

'*Ji wuahumi*, relax. Rick is delivering the camp bed.'

'Yeah when? After he's called the cops and you're in jail? Much safer and cosier in my house. Come with me. I got spare keys.'

'You're very kind, but that would require your father's permission.'

'It's OK, he wouldn't mind.'

'You must speak to him. And anyway, what about the neighbour who called the police?'

'Mrs Scully? We'll tell her you're – let's think – Da's nephew, me first cousin!'

'African nephew? African cousin? You better think of something better.'

I climb on me bike. 'You think this is going to work, Fifi?'

Shrugs and smiles. 'I don't know. But it will be interesting, don't you think?'

'Guess what, Fifi? Auntie Gracie's invited you for coffee.'

'Oh, how nice. But what about your . . . ?'

'Me uncle won't be there.'

'Well then, tell her I'd be delighted.'

First Kiss

Gives me the heebie-jeebies coming here, but Geri May's buzzing.

'We're early, Hop, let's scoot through the really bad wards, A and E and Cancer and Intensive Care. Say we've got relations.'

'What for?'

'All that blood and tubes and busted bones, don't you just love it?'

There's no saying no to Geri May. She'd have had Jesus ordering pizzas in the wilderness. So we moon around like ghouls in all the worst places till we get chased out or moved on.

At last me da's ward, where she pulls me behind a coffee machine and puts a Bounty Bar to me throat.

'I've no mobile,' I choke, 'and me trainers are worthless.'

'Bite!'

'I'd like to, but—'

'Then do it.'

'You know I can't, Geri May.'

'Will you do it for a kiss?'

'What?'

'Take a bite and I'll give you a kiss.'

'I don't know, after what you called me this morning.'

'What did I call you?'

'I don't even want to think it.'

'Oh yeah, I remember, I didn't mean it.'

She's on her tippy toes, her face in mine, disgusting strawberry chewing-gum in her breath and a whitehead like a jewel on her nose – will I tell her? Reminds me of the time Mam and Da had a fight before Mass and I combed me hair in a panic, and wondered why I was getting all these funny looks in church, till I got home and found the comb still in me hair.

'What d'you say, Hop, a bite for a kiss?'

I'm looking at her lips. I've never kissed a girl before, certainly none as pretty as Scary Mary, not even in me dreams. Me knees are knocking, I'm cross-eyed.

'OK.'

She smiles. She knew she'd win.

'Only can I have the kiss first?' I beg.

'You drive a hard bargain, Hopper Rooney,' she says, and stretches and kisses me. I was afraid she might trick me with a cheeky peck, but I get the full dry snakeskin rub of her mouth on mine. It lasts about four seconds, but

154

it's worth a million Bounties. I've had good times with Da and Mam and Deano; I've had great war games in me room and brilliant crashes on me bike, but this beats all.

Now the punishment.

She's unwrapping the bar, lifting it to me nose so I get a shocking whiff of choccy. Then just when I open me mouth to bite, she pulls back and pops it in her own mouth.

'It's OK, you don't have to,' she says, 'I hate the stink of sick.'

We go looking for Da. I'm so stunned by the kiss I have to beat me brain to remember the plan is NOT to tell him the whole story. We agreed on the bus we don't want to hurt him with promises.

I stop dead.

'What's wrong?' she goes.

Someone's being wheeled out on a trolley, skin and bone and eyes screwed tight. The trolley's coming closer. Geri May grabs me arm, me mind runs wild. I'm at the funeral in a suit ten sizes too small. Mam's there, and Frank her fancy feller . . .

Closer still and me heart kicks again. Nothing like Da.

'It's OK, it's not him.'

'Holy mackerel,' goes Geri May, 'you frit me to death!'

A voice behind us. 'Hopper?'

Spin round. Here he comes in that silky

boxer's dressing-gown Mam got him ninety-two Christmases ago, shuffling and grinning, chuffed as a bag of chips.

'Look at your old da! I'm doing great, one for the record books.'

He looks terrible, thin as a pin and bald as a chicken, and I can feel Geri May's shock in me arm.

'And who's this – new girlfriend?'

Geri May lets go – the blood flies to me face.

'Da, I'm only twelve. This is Geri May.'

'Geri May! You've grown up so, I didn't know you.'

'Hi, Uncle Eddie, how you doing? You're looking great.'

I love Geri May with all me heart and soul.

'Come on, you guys, let's take a stroll. Hopper tells me you're hot at science and computers.'

'Hopper's full of bull, Uncle.'

'Test you! What's copper nitrate? – Police overtime! What d'you get if you swallow uranium? – Atomic ache! Or as the Martian said to the customs officer, "We landed by mistake, we didn't planet this way!" Ha!'

He whistles as he walks us to a canteen of bright plastic tables and says, 'What're you having? Treat yourselves!'

'I'm not that hungry, Da.'

'Nonsense!'

'We just had dinner.'

'Then have a Coke or something.'

156

'Not for me, Da.'

''Course, silly me! How about you, kiddo?'

'I'll have what he has, Uncle Eddie.'

'Vodka and lime for me, Da.'

He looks at me, smiles. Like old times. 'I think we better make that three orange juices!'

'Want me to get them?' offers Geri May.

'Hey, come on, guys, I'm not that sick.'

We watch him go. 'Didn't mean to upset him,' says Geri May.

'Da's always been the rock of me life. Now look at him.'

He comes back all smiles.

'Here, Da, I brought your post – and some Marmite!'

'And me ma sent bananas to build you up,' says Geri May, 'and two cartons of your favourite grapefruit juice.'

'You're stars, pair of you,' he says, out of breath.

'Da?'

'What?'

'Have they found out anything yet?'

He hesitates. I feel Geri May still as ice beside me.

'Yes they have,' says Da, 'and I'm getting the best treatment.'

'What is it? Is it serious? You coming home soon?'

'Put it this way, they've caught it in time and

157

I'll be home, maybe not soon, but soon after. Dry your eyes, son, I'm proud of you.'

Geri May's hand's on me shoulder, like the girl you've secretly married with a toy ring and home-made confetti. First her lips, now her hand. What a day.

Da bends to pick up his napkin and Geri May digs me in the ribs – *ouch!* That hurt. It's time to mention the garage.

'Da, a few of us have been going in sweeping and tidying, checking the locks and getting your overalls cleaned.'

'You serious?'

'So it'll be ready for you, when you get out.'

He looks shocked.

'Aren't you glad?' says Geri May.

'You've taken me by surprise,' he whispers. 'I don't know what to say.'

'Say you're happy, Da.'

'I'm happy.'

'And guess what, Ambrose is helping.'

'Ambrose?'

'And Peach.'

'What?'

'You know, Peter—'

'I know who Peach is,' he snaps. 'What's he doing in the garage?'

Hold me breath and look down.

'We all want to help, Uncle Eddie,' says Geri May. 'We don't want the past, you know – to go on for ever.'

158

'Don't tell me me long-lost brother's ready to forgive?'

'We haven't told him.'

'You guys are playing with fire.'

'You don't mind us going in then, Uncle?'

'No, Geri May, I'm grateful.'

Geri May's looking eyes at me, trying to tell me something. How could I forget? Da's looking wrecked, but I have to ask.

'Da, there's something else . . .'

'Hey, look at the time. Walk me back, will youse?'

We walk either side of him, Eddie Rooney's heavies.

'I made a new friend, Da, a Simon seeker, and he's helping too.'

'A what?'

'You know, a Simon seeker.'

'Simon seeker? Asylum seeker, ye fool!' he roars, laughing.

On to Da's room, where he gets into bed and lies back, burned out.

'You OK, Da?'

'Not a bother, son. Just overdone it a bit.'

'This feller Fifi's been living rough, and I told him – I mean, I was wondering if it's OK he stays in our house for a bit?'

The question hangs like a balloon in the breeze from the window overlooking a field they're filling with all the same houses.

'How old's this—?'

'Fifi. Seventeen.'

'He's real growed up and sound,' says Geri May.

Da gazes out of the window, thinking of Mam, his garage, his life . . . 'I'll have to trust you on this,' he whispers. 'We go to Mass and say our prayers and sometimes forget we're Christians. Jesus was a refugee, after all. Never a day's peace.'

'But Mrs Scully, Da, she called the cops when I let him sleep in the shed.'

'Tell her it's OK.'

'He made a great job of the beds, Da. Will I bring you some of the carrots and stuff he's growing?'

'Thanks for coming. Grace will be wondering where you are.'

Geri May pulls me away. I break free.

'Da, what would you say if by some miracle we got the garage going again?'

He gives a sleepy wave and closes his eyes.

Out in the corridor we run for the exit.

'What do you reckon he's got?' I ask, chasing her down the stairs.

'I don't know, Hopper.'

Whatever we think it is, we're not saying.

Secret VIP for Tea

Tension rising like Auntie's pressure cooker –
me and Auntie, Peach and Geri May all chewed
up wondering what to do, cos Fifi's coming
any minute and Uncle Maddy's still here. He
was supposed to be seeing a dealer, but the
man cancelled and Uncle's home, hanging
around like a bad smell, sagging on the sofa
with Auntie watching *Fair City*, her nearly
favourite soap, just pipped by *Coronation
Street* which she wouldn't miss if the house was
on fire.

'You hate this, honey,' says Auntie, 'why
don't you slip away with Peach for a pint?'

'Take a crane to lift me, love.'

'Or a flash of Kylie Minogue's legs?'

'Mmm,' goes Uncle, 'think she might be
behind the bar tonight?'

'For sure, hon, if she thought there was a
hope of serving you.'

The week is drifting by and the garage is still

dead and Fifi's going to walk in any minute and get a faceful of Uncle Maddy, Grand Rooster of the Ballybriggan branch of the Ku Klux Klan.

Think positive! Uncle could have a heart attack before Fifi gets here, and anyway, we're doing our best. The flyers should have cost a packet, but Paddy Cassidy, the printer, says Da's a good man and done them for nothing. And Peach is handy with a paintbrush, and cobbled a sign saying GREAT NEWS! ROONEY'S MOTOR REPAIRS OPEN FOR BUSINESS! which Ambo waved like a flag for three whole days while I posted the flyers up and down the town.

It's been dodo ever since, Da's tinny old radio going non-stop in the office, Fifi polishing his spanners, Geri May playing games on her PC, and me and Ambo studying diagrams of engines, all waiting for the first car to turn into the yard.

Uncle stretches and yawns. He's getting up! He's not. He's slipping back again, eyes heavy.

'Peach, hon, what time's Father Brennan coming round?' says Auntie all of a sudden.

'What?' goes Peach, not getting it.

'Father Brennan . . .' Auntie repeats, firing looks at him.

Uncle's eyes pop like eggs. He's allergic to priests.

'Should be here any sec' – Geri May, quick as a light!

'Jeepers!' Uncle leaping like a fish. 'I'm parched.'

I hold me breath. Peach grabs Uncle's hat. Uncle slaps his pockets.

'Rats! Where's me wallet?'

'Leave it, Da, it's on me,' says Peach, holding the door.

Me and Geri May fly to the window. He's gone – we're saved!

We're not! Here's Fifi walking up from the bus. Peach sees him and suddenly finds a wasp or something on Uncle's jacket, distracting him while Fifi glides by. Close!

The bell rings. Auntie checks herself in the mirror and answers it. Puts out her hand. 'Pleased to meet you, Kofi.'

'Fifi, please. And it's my pleasure, Mrs Rooney.'

'Grace, please. And the pleasure's all mine.'

'Jeez!' goes Geri May. 'Will youse two stop pleasuring!'

Grace and Fifi still holding hands, love at first sight.

'Do sit down, Fifi, make yourself at home. I've heard such nice things about you.'

'I've heard even nicer things about you, Grace.'

'Oh my God,' goes Geri May.

'What can I get you, Fifi? Coffee, beer – peppermint tea?'

'Peppermint tea would be very nice indeed.'

Catch Fifi's eye. He smiles. I can relax now, *si abotre*, take it easy.

I hope.

Fufu for Fifi

Sitting on the doorstep waiting for Fifi, when Mrs Scully pops out of her front door. 'Is that you, Hopper?'

No, it's Mickey Mouse! 'Yes, Mrs Scully.'

'What are you doing?'

'Waiting for the new lodger, Mrs Scully.'

'Lodger?' she goes, like I said waiting for the rat-catcher.

'Me da doesn't like the house empty.'

'And what about the garden? It's a jungle again.'

'Mr Ford's going to do it.'

'Who?'

'The new lodger.'

Poor woman's panicking. Afraid of living next to riff-raff.

'What's he do, this Mr . . . ?'

'He's, um, an engineer,' says I, 'real good ear for engines.'

A taxi pulls up. Out steps Fifi – in a suit! And tie! Wow!

'Is *this* him?'

'Yes, Mrs Scully. He's the nephew of the boss of the Ford Motor Company, and he's very, very rich.'

Kids in the street stop their games and stare. No-one darker than a suntan has ever stepped out of a cab in Halpin Drive.

'Are ye famous, mister?'

'Are you on telly?'

'D'you know Tiger Woods?'

Fifi says hellos and smiles. I hold the broken gate, take his suitcase and shake his hand.

'You must be Hopper Rooney,' he goes. 'My uncle sends kind regards, and hopes you can visit us in Detroit.'

'Mr Ford, meet my good neighbour, Mrs Scully.'

'My privilege,' says Fifi, skipping over to the fence and stretching out a hand.

Mrs Scully wipes her hand on her apron and offers it, her face confused, charmed – suspicious.

I take him inside, show him round. 'This is your home, Fifi, till me da gets out. You can cook what you want and have it watching telly. What's your favourite meal when you want to feel at home?'

'Fufu.'

'Fufu? What's fufu?'

'You make it with yam, plantain or cassava, or with all three, peeled and sliced, boiled and

166

pounded and served with palm nut oil. I'll make it for you some day.'

'Sounds disgusting. But I'll give it a try. And look, if you get bored . . .'

I take him upstairs, uncover the war games table and unveil me legions of warriors.

'We could play together,' says I. 'After our fufu.'

A stone or something hits the window in the front bedroom. Sounds like trouble. I won't stand for it! I'll kill anyone who says or does anything to hurt me friend.

With fists clenched and gritted teeth I run to the front room ready to hurl down every filthy insult I know – and stop! *Ji wuahumi*, relax, it's only Gork-Sergeant Slugs, looking up like an eejit. Open the window.

'Is it him?'

'*Shhh!*'

'Can I meet him?'

''Course you can.'

Mission Impossible

Days are flying by, Peach has joined us and nothing's doing. I knew this would never work. We've posted millions more flyers in doors, and billions more on car windscreens, and still nothing.

Our flyer-posting beat takes us dangerously close to Crazy Prices.

'What do you say, Ambo, we breeze in and snatch a bar of gold?'

This is your last, last, LAST warning, said good old Alro Redlips.

'You're right, Ambo, it wouldn't do to get nicked now and hauled before the International War Crimes Triangle.'

But it's tempting.

Days drag. I pass the time studying repair manuals, Ambo plays with a tool box he's made his own, Peach and Fifi knock a ball around without a word, and Geri May sits by the phone reading teen mags with gems like

SURE WAYS TO MAKE YOURSELF IRRESISTIBLE and TEN THINGS YOU NEVER KNEW ABOUT KISSING. I get sick watching her read that stuff.

Waste of time. I could be playing war games with Fifi – Starlord Kofi against the Dregs of Asterdoon.

And then, just when we're least expecting it and I'm praying for a meteorite to wipe out the garage, the street and the whole world, a car bumps along the lane and turns into the yard – by mistake, I suppose, looking for a picnic spot. Peach and Fifi freeze, staring at the guy like it's Jesus making his comeback in our lowly garage.

Then I recognize Mr Goggins's Stone-Age Mazda, and out hops the man himself saying, 'Got your flyer. Where's Eddie? How's he doing?'

The next minute the phone rings and Geri May nearly jumps out of her skin, picks it up and says, 'Yeah, what do you want?'

We're in business.

Fifi works fast. The Mazda's a mess, but he's happy, we all are, and stand around watching, throwing glances at the gate, cos any second now another car's going to roll in, and another . . .

Bring us your motors,
Ladies and gents!

169

Yer Rollers and Rovers.
And Mercedes Benz.

Bring 'em in battered
And rusty and blue.
We'll give 'em back
Mended and shiny and new!

Hours fly by, Fifi shows me and Peach how to beat out dents and rub out rust while he untangles the Mazda's engine, and all of a sudden we look up and the sun's falling and the yard's empty.

Our hearts droop.

'One customer all day,' laughs Peach. 'What a joke.'

'It's that Robber Baron's fault!' I cry out, and they all look at me like I've cracked.

'What robber baron?' goes Peach.

'Robert Barry Motors, he's got big and flash since Da closed. Each time I go by, he's bigger and busier.'

'Right!' goes Peach. 'I'm going round first thing, tell him I'll burn him out if he doesn't give us our trade back.'

'With respect, Peter,' says Fifi, 'perhaps we should send someone to talk to him first.'

Why are they all looking at me?

'OK, give us the phone book,' says Peach. 'I'll call him.'

'No you won't,' says Geri May, 'that's my department.'

We ride home in gloom, Ambo clinging to Peach, me tailing free-wheeling Geri May, who's way past her curfew, but that's OK – her da keeps his shop open late to trap tourists and doesn't get in till eight.

Fall exhausted into bed. Me first day as a car mechanic.

'You and me, Ambo, they're sending us round in the morning to tackle me da's arch-enemy, the Robber Baron of Ballybriggan. Better go armed – what d'you say?'

Ambo looks up from a jigsaw he's done so often, Auntie's had to sellotape nearly all the pieces.

'Water pistols? Paper aeroplanes, pea-shooters? Take yer pick.'

Me roommate answers with a rattly noise in his gizzard.

'Machine-guns in violin cases – great idea, Ambo.'

I sleep easier thinking of Fifi tucking into fufu in me da's kitchen at home, and then sleeping cosy in my bed. But me nerves are hopping thinking about tomorrow . . .

It's a hot sticky morning. Winds must have taken a wrong turn and swung in from the

Sahara. I'm sweating and Ambo's hanging his tongue like a dog.

Armed with a sackful of flyers, we approach Robert Barry Motors on foot. It's a busy beehive, millions of men working on millions of cars lured in with fluttering flags and Special Offers spinning in the wind.

I'm dressed in best trainers, shirt and jumper, with Ambo in an Umbro tracksuit, tied to me wrist like a convict.

Mr Barry knows we're here, but keeps us waiting, and waiting and waiting. His secretary has a fan blowing cool air in her face and warm air in ours. On the wall's a boasty sign saying, ROBERT BARRY MOTORS USES THE LATEST COMPUTER-ENHANCED DIAGNOSIS TO FIX YOUR CAR! Handy, I suppose, if you haven't noticed the fuel gauge is empty.

'Send 'em in, Marie!' yer man calls.

Da's enemy is a big red-faced feller in a classy suit, like a farmer that just scooped the Lotto. Munching on a mayonnaisey sandwich, he reaches over to shake and nearly break me hand.

'You must be Eddie Rooney's boy. And, em, who's this?'

He's uneasy about Ambo. Can see something's wrong with him, but what? And why's he here?

'This is Ambrose. Me lawyer.'

'Ha!' yer man laughs, spraying scraps of bread. 'A regular comedian. Sit down, but don't get comfy, I'm a busy man.'

172

I drag two chairs together, we sit, and I'm about to start when the phone goes.

'Excuse me,' he says, and gets into a knotty argument about a hefty bill, which ends with him advising the caller to take his custom elsewhere.

'Sorry about that,' he says, 'what can I do for you?'

'Me da's business, Mr Barry. We're getting it going again and—'

Phone goes. 'Excuse me,' he says, and gets into another scuffle with a customer which ends like the first with the phone slammed down. 'Sorry, lads, where were we?'

'It's like this, Mr Barry, Da lost customers to you when he got sick—'

Phone again! This time it's not even business, he's leaning back having a natter with a pal. When he's done, he hangs up with a laugh and says, 'You boys still here?'

'About our lost customers, Mr Barry, any chance you could—'

I was going to say, send some of them over to us, but there it goes again, Mr Alexander Graham Bell's blinkin' blower, and this time yer man's nearly stretched out for an even longer wag with his missus about who's coming to dinner, and why don't they grab a week in the Canaries and where could he have lost his club tie!

Hangs up, yawns and checks his watch.

'Time's up,' he goes, coming round to usher us out.

'But Mr Barry, you haven't – we haven't—'

'Nothing I can do, son. Sorry about your old man, but business is business, *c'est la vie*. Thanks for coming. Good luck.'

Me and Ambo, standing in the dusty sun like a couple of cans tossed from a car. I've never felt so small. Wish Geri May was with us. She'd have given him an earful. They should never have sent me. It was like putting Tinky Winky in the ring with Mike Tyson. I want to go home, I want me mam.

Then I get this rush of rage, like me brains are going to blow.

'Scumbag, he's not getting rid of us that easy, Ambo.'

We place ourselves at the gate, and any driver that comes near gets a Hopper Rooney smile and a flyer. Two flyers – as many as you want.

'And tell your friends, mister, my da does the same job better, quicker and cheaper!'

I get plenty of smiles back, and the odd blast of abuse, and a pretty blonde lady in a soft-top Astra who reads the flyer and goes, 'Oh, Eddie's open, that's wonderful news!' and U-turns away with a friendly wave.

And so it goes, any driver I can catch, customer or not – 'And we do the same job quicker, cheaper and better!' – till I feel a hand on me shoulder: the Grim Reaper.

Yer man himself with a big smile.

'Oh, hello, Mr Barry.'

'Still here, lads! Can't find your way home? Allow me.'

'Hang on a sec,' I'm saying, but he has me and Ambo by the arm and he's shifting us like a couple of refuse bags into a back lane jammed with dumped junk and empty skips. Wham! – pins me against a wall. The smile's whipped off and swapped for a scary stare.

'Don't let me see your face round here again, understood?'

'I'll have you for assault,' I hear meself squeak.

'What did you say?'

'Pass the salt!'

'I never laid a hand on you,' he goes, pinning me harder.

'Ambo's me witness.'

'Him?' he laughs, and he's still laughing as he screws up one of our flyers, flings it in a skip and walks away.

I'm shaking. Ambo's shaking and upset and going, 'Fay-fay-fay!'

'It's OK, Ambo, it's OK. Wait till I tell me da! Wait till we tell Peach!'

On second thoughts, Da would only get upset, and Peach might come round and do something crazy.

GARAGE OWNER BEATEN TO DEATH WITH PINEAPPLE.

'Come on, Ambo, let's go.'

It's good to be back. There's Fifi working on Blondie's soft-top Astra, and here's all the gang gathering round to see how we got on.

'He wasn't interested. Business is business, *say la vie.*'

'Did he treat you bad?' says Peach, spiked pineapple behind his back.

'No, he was real nice, wasn't he, Ambo? But he won't be sending us spare business, that's for sure.'

It's not all hopeless. We got the Astra Fifi's servicing for its test, and in the afternoon Geri May gets a run of three calls from potential customers who must have seen our flyers, so things are brightening up!

Sheriff Rooney Blows His Nose

At least they *were* brightening up. Then the worst thing that could possibly happen happens – worse than a meteorite, worse than a plague of cobras.

We lock up, and say bye to Fifi, who sets off jogging to Mrs Quincy's. Peach and Ambo scoot off on the bike, and me and Geri May follow in no particular hurry and get home to find something parked outside the house that shouldn't be there – not at around half-six. Uncle Maddy's car! *Holy Hubcaps!*

We skid to a stop. I look at Geri May. The blood's gone from her face. Me heart bangs like a bell.

Ever hear of Bonnie and Clyde,
The terrible way they died.
Hopper and Geri also wed,
Pulled pranks, robbed banks
And wound up dead.

'I'm not going in,' she says.

'What else can we do?'

'Fly to the moon, run away to London, anything.'

'What if we sneak in and up the stairs?'

She's thinking about it. Nods – yep, not a bad idea. She leads with the key. Opens the door real quiet and in we go like a couple of thieves into the teeny entrance hall and up the stairs to safety. Least that's the plan, only the living-room door's wide open – why shouldn't it be? – and there he is, the ugliest sheriff you ever saw, sitting in a corner waiting for us, hat down over his eyes like an avenger. Auntie and Peach are sat hushed on the sofa like naughty kids. Ambo's out of range somewhere.

Uncle's head is down – maybe he's asleep.

Like we've practised it, me and Geri May start taking incy-wincy steps towards the stairs . . .

'Where do you two think you're going?'

We freeze together. Look at each other, each hoping the other might have a way out.

Uncle Maddy lifts his head, eyes coming up under his hat like the barrels of a gun. 'Get in here and sit down.'

We go in. Geri May looks at Auntie, her eyes saying, *What's he doing home?*

The furthest spot from where he's sitting is the spare armchair, so me and Geri May squeeze in together, which any other time would be brilliant, her thigh trembling against mine.

No-one speaks. We're sinners in the sight of God, even Auntie looking sorry, hands in lap. Uncle looking at me – no-one else, just me. He's got a piece of paper he's smoothing out in his hand like a shocking letter. Only it's not a letter, it's one of me flyers.

'I'm surprised at you, Hopper,' he says, low and grisly. 'I thought you were an honest boy.'

He's gazing at me more hurt than mad, like the hustler in one of his movies who can't believe his buddy's double-crossed him.

'It's not the pain your father's caused me, Hopper. I've lived with that for twelve years, and as your Aunt Grace never tires of telling me, it was my fault for playing fast and loose with the garage's capital. You know about this, don't you?'

Nod.

'That said, he had no business kicking me out, threatening me with the law – your da's a hard man behind the pally front.'

I can hear gloomy organ music and a funeral choir. Three members of the same family, plus a young cousin called Hopper, dead in mingling pools of blood – only the disabled son Ambrose mysteriously spared.

'No it's not any of that, Hopper. I don't have a problem with you trying to salvage your da's

179

garage – even if it is, by rights, mine too. I admire you for it. And I don't object to you roping me son and daughter into your little scheme. Makes sense. You couldn't do without them. And if you want to use an African asylum seeker everyone says is a good, clean, hard-working boy, then work away.'

Now, as he looks at me, his eyes start to water and his voice turns croaky as a blocked drain.

'What upsets me is you've done all this behind me back. Conceived it, discussed it, carried it out. All of you – me wife, son, daughter and me brother's boy who I took into me house – all plotting behind me back.'

Nod.

'Why didn't you come to me, Hopper, tell me what was in your mind? Why didn't you all come to me?'

'I told you,' says Auntie, 'they were afraid.'

'Afraid? Me whole family? I grant you I lose me head from time to time, threaten to take a hand to one of youse, but when's the last time I done it? Can anyone remember – or were you still in nappies?'

He looks at us all real mad and wounded. The choir and organ sound sadder than ever. *Small-time antiques dealer found hanging in his shop in a Queen Anne grandfather clock, about 1700 – the clock, that is, not the time of death.*

'OK, I'd have made a stink, but I'm not an unreasonable man!'

'Aren't you?' says Auntie.

'Not given a chance.'

'Like we said, Da,' says Peach, 'we were going to tell you if the thing got going – and not tell if it didn't – so's not to upset you.'

'You're all forbidden from going anywhere near that garage, you hear!' he goes jumping to his feet and swiping the air, 'and you, Geri May, are grounded for another four weeks, ye scheming scut! You've disobeyed me, you've all cheated and disrespected me, and that's how I feel, that's what I wanted to say,' he says, suddenly soft and low again, 'but I've listened to Grace and Peach and they say it wouldn't be fair, it wouldn't be right . . .'

He stands leaning like a tree in a wind, nose sniffly and eyes watery, not knowing where to go next.

'So, do what you like, all of youse. Rescue the garage. Make my brother's day. If you all hate me so much, I may as well take meself out and get drunk!'

'I'll be in by five each day, Da, I promise!' goes Geri May.

'You won't, young lady, you'll be in any time you like, cos I don't give a monkey's!'

'*Map-map!*' goes a voice from the kitchen.

'You're *un*grounded, girl, cos I give up!' says Uncle, turning to the door.

181

'Don't say that!' says Geri May, popping up like a toaster and flinging herself in his way. 'I'm staying grounded and I'm sorry, Da, we should have told you!'

'Don't Da me, I've retired!' he shouts, pushing her away. 'I'm nobody's da no more.'

'You're my da, the only one I got!' she shrieks, throwing herself at him again.

'Get off me, I'm going out to get smashed!'

'Don't, Da, don't! I hate you smashed and we need you.'

'No you don't,' he goes, trying to wrestle her off. 'You want a da that lets you paint yer face and wear short skirts and do what you like. Nobody needs me, I'm out!'

He throws her off and reaches the door – she springs back and catches hold of him.

'Get off! I'm going! I give up!' he roars, trying to shake her off, but she's glued to him and won't let go, like a piece of newspaper in the wind, like a rat on a cat's neck.

He stops, exhausted. They stand back and stare at each other.

'Don't, Da, don't give up – *PLEEEEZE!*'

He droops, sighs.

'Please don't go, don't run away from us, you're a great da.'

'You don't mean that.'

'She does, you fool,' says Auntie.

Uncle lets Geri May lead him back to his

seat. 'You all hate me,' he says, looking at his boots.

'No we don't,' says Peach.

'You do, youse all do,' he wails.

Peach holds his head. Geri May starts blubbing.

'You know we love ye, Maddy,' says Auntie, real smooth and smoky, 'most of the time.'

He looks big and lost and lonely. I feel small and lost and lonely.

Auntie pats the sofa and says, 'Come over here, hon.'

The old gunslinger's wore out. Met his match in Geri May.

'Come on, get your big bum over here,' goes Auntie, getting up to fetch him over to the sofa, where Peach makes room for him.

Auntie hands him a hanky and we all look away while he wipes his nose. Then he looks up to find me.

'Does Eddie still hate me?'

The question catches me out. I'd like to say, *No, Uncle, I'm sure he really likes you deep down*, but lying's not me best event.

'Maybe it'll all get better now,' says I.

'Your brother's sick, hon,' says Auntie. 'Why don't you pay him a visit?'

'Are ye mad, woman?' goes Uncle and steps outside for a smoke.

*   *   *

It turns into a real quiet, strange, magical evening. The TV goes off after *Fair City*, Auntie and Uncle are sipping wine and Ambo curls up with a favourite jigsaw piece and falls asleep under the table, me and Geri May play a giggly game of Snap, and then another round so fierce we nearly come to blows, and Peach tucks himself away and calls the girl who ditched him, and returns with a grin on his face wide as a clown's.

Darkness falls, lights come on in the street, we step outside to where Auntie and Uncle are playing backgammon with a candle in a jar throwing red light on the step – me and Geri May in jim-jams and Peach in his bathrobe speaking for us.

'Just wanted to check it's still OK we go in tomorrow?'

'Go in where?' says Uncle.

'You know – the garage.'

'Oh, the garage?' He rattles the dice and blasts it off the board and down the steps. 'Sure, why not? What's it to me?'

Bed at last, cosy duvet – a little breeze in the window making Ambo's wind-chimes tinkle – voices murmuring outside, the clunk of an empty bottle on the hard step, the *pop!* of another one. Everything peaceful.

All kneel for the Jigsaw king

A brand new day, rain in the air, but who cares, we're flying!

So much to tell Fifi – 'You'll never know how close it came to curtains! He went mad, wanted to stop us coming anywhere near the garage, but Peach and Auntie talked him round, and guess what? Me big bad uncle cried! Nearly flooded the house.'

'Good for him,' says Fifi.

'It was real embarrassing.'

'No, why? I like a man who cries.'

'Do you cry, Fifi?'

He knows what I'm getting at and looks away.

'Did you lose many in your family, Fifi?'

'I write letters and wait for replies. They came in the night. I wasn't there, I was in Accra at the garage.'

'Who came in the night, Fifi?'

'Political enemies. People afraid of our culture and power.'

185

'What about your parents?'

He spreads his hands. He doesn't know. 'I believe some of my family are dead, and some may have escaped. But so far, no-one has replied.'

I look at the scar on his cheek and try to imagine how many others with that mark are alive, and how many are dead.

'They'll let you stay, Fifi, I know they will.'

He takes a newspaper from his pocket. Shows me the headline. TEN-MILLION-POUND BRIBE TO REPATRIATE REFUGEES! 'They want to pay African governments to take us back.'

'Scumbags. I'll talk to them! Better still, I'll send Geri May!'

Fifi laughs. He looks happy. Me heart sings.

'Will it help that you're needed by two – you know, employers – me da and Mrs Quincy?'

'Yes, I think so.'

A car's bumping along the lane, turning through the gate. Twenty minutes later, here comes another.

Holy hubcaps! A trickle's turning into a river! By afternoon we got five cars in the yard and six telephone enquiries. Old and new customers have heard the word, and from one minute to the next Fifi's busy, talking to drivers, making notes on Da's old clipboard, hopping from one engine to the next and giving me and Peach whatever little jobs he thinks we can handle – replacing bulbs and wipers, polishing spark-plugs – while Ambo, wearing a sideways baseball cap on his prickly head, follows him everywhere, eyes skinned.

Fifi gets funny looks. Old customers take me aside and ask for Da.

'Glad to hear he's better, but where is he?'

'Um . . . he's still in and out of hospital for rehab.'

'So who's this other feller?'

'Oh, Freddie, Da's new mechanic – best in the business. Flew him in from Detroit.'

The cars keep coming, three or four a day, limping in bashed and broken, or just rolling in for a service. Cars are funny yokes, so smooth and everlasting on telly, coasting through earthquakes and tornadoes without a scratch and never meeting traffic. But up close and robbed of gloss and glitter, even the poshest ones look common – designed by computers, built by robots, driven by eejits.

Da says you used to be able to recognize any car a mile off. Each model stood out in the crowd saying, *I'm me! I'm different*. Now the cops go crazy getting witnesses to say what the crook was driving, cos it doesn't matter if it's a Vectra or a Corsa, an Almera or a Primera, a Xantia, a Xsara, a Brava or a Laguna – they all have naff names and all look the same.

Motoring used to be an adventure. Now it's all huff and puff.

'How soon will it be ready?'

'Ooh,' goes Fifi, 'two or three days.'

'Two or three days? I need it tomorrow! Tonight!'

'I'll see what I can do, sir.'

The yard's filling up, Fifi's starting to overheat. The economy's jumping, the country's swimming in loot, everyone and his granny's got a car and they're all breaking down or slamming into each other, and some days Fifi never stops, out of one engine and into another. Some days he's so tired, he gets muddled and goes right back to the car he just fixed, like a surgeon opening up the same patient twice.

One day he boils over.

'Hopper, we can't go on like this.'

'What?' Me heart flips. 'What are you saying?'

'I can't keep up. We're doing too well. Customers are waiting too long and getting upset. And Peach is back in work tomorrow and you'll be in school soon.'

'You're not walking out on us, are you, Fifi?'

'No, my friend. Just get me more hands.'

'How? Where?'

'You're the boss. What do you suggest?'

'Um, let me think. Advertise? Yes, that's it, we'll advertise.'

188

The ad goes in and turns up all kinds of blokes, from experienced hands to shamsters who wouldn't know a spark-plug from a park slug. Fifi keeps working while he interviews them one by one late into the evening and early next day, till he's happy to hire a young feller covered in spiders and dragons called Spit, and a baldy old geyser called Rosco, who rubs oil into his skull and polishes it up every morning to make it glow.

Spit and Polish catch on real quick and start taking some of the strain.

Fifi's patient with me. I listen closely to his instructions and still get it wrong, putting wipers on backwards and getting lightbulbs I'm replacing mixed up.

'Sorry, Fifi, I'm hopeless.'

'*Si abotre,* my friend, you're doing—'

Just fine is what I hope he means to say, when something catches his eye and I look up and see it too – a sleek ghostly machine in the lane, caressing the cobbles and sweeping into the yard with a face everyone knows at the wheel and the world gleaming in his hub-caps. He's a little old guy with a squirrely face who nearly needs a highchair to see over the dashboard.

His Merc's a real pearl. Late sixties, early seventies. You see them in old films but seldom in the street – soft lines and smooth angles, solid-looking but warm, elegant but not in your face, a real beaut that catches you in the throat and makes you dream.

The number plate says CRYSTAL 1. Mr Crow lost his wife years ago. Everyone knows him. He made his money in Venetian blinds, but never left the area and never let it go to his head.

'Where's Eddie, young man?'

'I'm sorry, he's not here today, sir,' goes Fifi.

'Well, I'm sure he has to take it easy. Tell him Johnny Crow's delighted he's up and running again. I don't like dragging the car into town, so I took her to that fellow on the roundabout – what's his name?'

'Robert Barry Motors,' says I, remembering with a shiver me little run-in with the Grim Reaper.

'That's the one, and they charged me a leg and an arm to make her worse. She's a dear old thing, and I hate to see her suffer.'

'What seems to be the trouble?' says Fifi.

'She's not running well,' says the old man, worried sick. 'Her old heart's tired and she can't shake off a nasty cough.'

'Sounds like she needs a thorough examination and some tender loving care,' says Fifi.

'That's what I was hoping you'd say.'

Fifi pushes other work onto Spit and Polish, and concentrates on the Merc. At first he's delighted to be handling such a classy machine, but soon he's racking his brains. Modern engines are neatly boxed with handy loops and tubes, but this one's complicated, wires everywhere, and Fifi's a little out of his depth and has to dig through Da's dusty handbooks to find a Merc close enough in age and design to Crystal. He lays the book with the diagram open on a stool.

Ambo's spellbound. Each time Fifi goes to check the diagram, the book's gone! Ambo's taken it to his oil-drum perch to study it.

'Ambo!' says I. 'How can Fifi work if you keep nicking the picture?'

Fifi has Crystal jacked up high so he can get underneath. Then he brings her down again to look in the engine, and as he pokes and sighs, Ambo pokes and sighs too, squinting over his shoulder.

Geri May yells from the office, 'It's Johnny Crow again, you wanna talk to him?'

Fifi takes a deep breath and goes to the phone, me and Geri May listening in.

'How's the patient doing?'

'Doing fine, sir, we'll get there.'

'How's her heart?'

'Heart's good.'

'Pulse?'

'So is her pulse. But something's still wrong and I haven't found it.'

'Don't give up on her, young man.'

'I won't.'

It's upsetting Fifi. Upsetting us all. He's

191

tested everything he can think of and he still can't say what's wrong with her.

'Come on, guys, fingers crossed!' says Fifi, climbing behind the wheel, and me and Ambo jump in the back and belt up and away we go for a spin. And what do you know! It's fine, running smooth!

'You've done it, Fifi!'

But he hasn't. Soon as we hit the main road – splutter-splutter, Crystal's coughing like an old girl who's had too many whiskeys and ciggies.

Fifi takes another call from Johnny Crow, and towards evening another.

'I'm sorry to bother you again, young man . . .'

'That's quite all right, sir, but I'm afraid I haven't any good news. I keep thinking she's trying to tell me where to look, but I just can't find it. Perhaps you should take her to a specialist.'

'You're probably right,' says the old man, 'but could you bear to keep trying tomorrow?'

We're all in the dumps, and I haven't seen Fifi look so whacked as he jogs away to Chapelizod. And me and Geri May are too banjaxed when we get home to do anything but eat and fall into bed.

Ambo's in great form, sitting up late, throwing dozens of jigsaws in the air all at once, and tackling them all together. I can't watch, it's too crazy.

Another warm and sticky day in Da's recuperating garage. Spit and Polish are teamed up on a brand new Saab that looks like it's been trampled by elephants, and Fifi's hard at work on the old Merc.

Ambo runs to join him.

'Morning, Ambrose! And how's my trusty partner today?'

Ambo's high and wired – diving into Crystal's engine like he means to throw all the parts in the air and start again.

'Ambo, *si abotre* – take it easy!' says I, running.

'It's OK,' says Fifi. 'Maybe he'll bring me luck.'

'Luck? He'll—' *Wreck it*, I was going to say, but I've hit oil on the floor and I'm slipping and sliding and *wham!* – whack me face on the Merc's glossy bumper. 'Sorry, Fifi, sorry,' says I, wiping away a smear of blood from the car with me sleeve.

'It's my fault, I should have cleaned the floor,' goes Fifi, picking me up and dusting me down.

It's only a small cut under me eye, but Fifi sits me down, finds a clean rag and water and pats it gently. Geri May comes out to look and I stop going *Ouch* to impress her, and Spit and Polish shuffle over to debate whether I'll need stitches.

Just then Ambo throws the repair manual on the floor.

'Better see what he's doing,' somebody says.

'Come here to us, Ambo,' says Rosco. 'Help us fix the Saab.'

Ambo's not listening, he's too busy in Crystal's engine, fingers working like crazy and mouth going, 'Goddy – goddy – goddy!'

'Jaysus, stop him, someone!'

'It's OK,' says Fifi. 'He can't make her any worse.'

'Goddy-goddy-goddy!'

I know that look on his face from when he's getting worked up finishing a tricky puzzle. He's either lost his head or he's onto something.

You have to laugh. 'He's saying he's nearly got it, Fifi.'

We all hover round, ready to drag Ambo clear, but Ambo's not tearing Crystal's guts out, he's working real careful. He's seen something in the diagram and he's found a wire he's not happy about. He's getting mad, he can't reach it.

Fifi's tucked in beside him.

'Let me try, Ambrose. This one, is it?'

'Goddy-goddy . . .'

It's done. One teeny weenchy wire.

Fifi gently closes the engine, looks at us, looks at Ambo, shrugs to Heaven. 'OK, gentlemen, let's go.'

We pile back into the Merc, me and Ambo in the back. Round and round the block we go, and once more for luck, the Merc gliding on air, purring like a lion, me catching Fifi's eye in the mirror, each of us throwing glances at Ambo, who's humming to himself, forgotten all about it already. Just another puzzle to old Ambo – all the way to Johnny Crow's house.

The old man comes out of his door looking worried. Thinks we've given up on the old girl.

'I think she's cured,' says Fifi.

'You mean . . . ?'

The old man falls on the car and weeps. 'Thank you, thank you!' wiping his eyes.

'Don't thank me, sir,' says Fifi. 'This is the young man who saw what no-one else could see.'

'And what's this genius's name?'

'The Jigsaw King!' says I, clapping me cousin on the back.

Johnny Crow invites us into his big lonely house and pours iced juice and gets out his cheque book. 'You've made an old man very happy. Name your price!'

Fifi looks at me and I look at Fifi.

'It's on the house, sir,' says Fifi.

'Compliments of Rooney Motor Repairs,' says I.

High Noon

Summer's over. Auntie's pressed me uniform and me school bag's packed.

Today is all that's left, and what a day it's going to be here at the garage! It was Auntie's idea, and everyone's invited. Me and Geri May made out the invites, including customers old and new, and Paddy Cassidy ran them off for free. On the garage gate hangs Peach's poster – ROLL UP FOR THE GRAND REOPENING OF ROONEY'S MOTOR REPAIRS! Prizes for the tombola include a massive hamper of fruit.

The rain's dying out, Peach gets the barbecue going and we carry trestle tables out the workshop into the yard and pile them high with cakes and pies, soft drinks, beer and wine – nearly all stuff I can't have without throwing a wobbly, so Auntie's made me a cake free of naughties which looks a treat but tastes of polystyrene.

It's possible the Press is sending someone over, so we remind each other that Fifi isn't

196

Fifi, he's Freddie, and he's not African, he's a Yank with a work permit. I'm coaching him how to say things like *Sure, buddy, no sweat buddy, you betcha bottom dollar, buddy!* so he sounds real American. And now someone's come up behind me and put their arms round me, and guess who it is? Freddie himself, whispering in me ear.

'Did you ever think you'd see this day – old buddy?'

I turn and look into me friend's eyes and I want to thank him from the bottom of me heart, but me throat's blocked by a boulder and me eyes are stinging and all Fifi can do is hold me while I sob like an eejit.

People are arriving – like wasps to jam, what did I say? The place is filling up and I'm standing on an oil drum watching the lane, waiting for a very special VIP.

What if he doesn't come? What if he dies on the way over in the cab? Oh God, me life's a mess. Mam can't make it – but said she'd phone – Da's dead or dying or crippled for life, and all I do is get in people's way, untidy their lives, get everything wrong and fail every mission they send me on . . . except this rescue mission, this brilliant day.

Me fingers go to me face and feel the little scar high on the cheek under the eye, nearly the same size and place as Fifi's scar. Every day in school this term, I'm going to touch that scar

197

and tell meself I'm not hopeless. I did it, *I did it!* I found the man who saved me daddy's garage.

Spit's here with Dee, his all-in-black Druid girlfriend, beautiful eyes caged in black make-up, beer glass held by black claws; and Rosco's brought his wife and a string of grandchisslers with ribbons in their hair, and Johnny Crow's arrived in his gleaming Merc, and Blondie in her soft-top Astra, and Mr Goggins in his patched-up heap, and soon the place is swarming and Peach has his turntable set-up belting out music for anyone who wants to dance. Stacey's come, the one who ditched him and let herself be sweet-talked round again, a tall, pasty gum-chewing doll who keeps telling him to leave out the heavy stuff and play something decent like Destiny's Child.

Ambo's insisted on wearing his greasy overalls and skewy cap, and he's wandering round hand in hand with Fifi – I mean Freddie – who looks the business in his suit and tie. A couple of geysers from the *Herald* are tucking into whatever's left, still asking awkward questions and still getting the same answers no matter who they talk to – he's Freddie Ford, from Detroit, helping out till Eddie's back in the groove.

And look who's here! Ellen Quincy and Sticky Rickie in his poncy BMW, Fifi stepping over to open her door – and what's this? A taxi in the lane! Me heart races. Could it be the guest I'm waiting for, the main man, the man himself?

He's made it!

I jump down and run. I want to open the door before he does, but he sees me and beats me to it, ducking out of the cab and standing up straight. He's wonky on his pins, cheesy white and short of hair, but he's still handsome, me da, looking at me and at the crowds that have gone quiet, and up at the sign that says his garage is now officially open.

He starts to reach for me. For a second I think he's falling and wants me to catch him, and then I see. No – he wants to lift me in his arms and stops himself, realizing he hasn't the strength.

The crowd breaks into applause, Da puts his arm round me shoulder and the Sea of Galilee parts for us – Da and his spoofer son who came good when it mattered. People are shaking hands with him, some have gone foreign and are hugging him. He wants to get up on a table. People are trying to stop him, but Rooneys are a stubborn breed, so we are, and with the help of a thousand hands he climbs up like Moses on the Mount, and for a minute he can't speak, he's all choked up, and a kind of soppy *ahhh* goes through the crowd, cos there's no bigger winner than a gonner who somehow bounces back. Then he looks like he's going to fall – the crowd gasps, hands grab his legs and he laughs out loud. Some party that would have

199

made, the chief guest breaking his neck.

I'm too worried the table's going to collapse or they're going to let him fall to catch much of his speech, only snatches that will stay with me for ever . . .

'All the time I been in hospital I never dreamed my son and his cousins and friend were coming in every day – not to tidy up like they told me first – but to work together to rebuild me business . . . I'm like the racehorse-owner who thought his horse was confined to stables terminally sick, only to wake up and hear it's gone and won the Gold Cup! . . . I admit it's been tough at times. Just when the economy's boiling and business is hot, I go and fall ill and wind up like the feller who dreams of limousines, but has nothing to chauffeur it! Ha! . . . My son Hopper's had it tough too – I'll never know how to thank him for all he's done to get this show back on the road . . .'

I'll always remember them lifting me on their shoulders and me dying of embarrassment, and Da calling for a glass and raising it high above the crowd to toast us. 'Let's hear it for the Rooney Motors Rescue Brigade! – my niece Geri May, nephews Peach and Ambrose, my boy Hopper and his friend and chief mechanic Freddie from Detroit – three cheers, hip hip!'

The roar of the crowd!

I'll never forget Da shaking hands with 'Freddie', and doing something I never seen him do before, open his arms and hug someone. And I'll never forget Fifi and Rick Quincy swapping a friendly nod in passing and better still, much better, Fifi and Peach bumping into each other in all the crush and spilling drinks, and for a terrible minute I'm thinking they're going to go for each other like dogs, only to see them laugh, and hear Fifi go, 'Thank you, Peter, for giving me a chance.'

'Don't mention it, Kofi. And in future, if you wanna know what's good for you, call me Peach.'

'Peach it will always be – provided you start calling me Fifi.'

'Well,' goes Peach, putting out his hand, 'this is as good a day as any. Congratulations, Fifi.'

The music starts up again, the party rolls and Da's in the office with me and Peach and Fifi inspecting the books when the phone rings and Geri May, in white jeans and silver jacket and her best posh voice, picks it up and goes, 'Rooney's Motor Repairs, Geri May speaking, how can I help you?' And guess what? Her eyes are popping, she's looking at me and mouthing *It's your ma!* and I'm nearly sick and can't get the words out fast enough telling her all what's happening and everyone who's here, including Bono and the Taoiseach and Madonna yakking with the Pope and Elvis!

Da wants to speak to her. He has to sit down, back in his old chair. They talk about me and how proud they are and then he says what I've been dying to hear and was afraid I'd never hear.

'I'll be out for Christmas . . . No, not back at work for at least six months, but that's OK, the garage is in good hands . . . Please God I'm clear for good and this nightmare's over . . . Great idea, Maggie, let's do it. Take care, God bless.' *Click*.

'What, Da, what's a great idea?'

'Your mam's coming over for your birthday. We're all going out.'

'Oh my God!' goes Geri May, looking out the window, and me heart stops, cos it has to be the cops come for Fifi. 'It's Ma and Da.'

I'm confused. Which ma? Whose da?

And then I twig, and we all look at my da, who knows his brother's arrived – the one he hasn't seen or spoken to in twelve years. No-one speaks. Me da gets up and goes to the door.

No parting of the waves for Uncle Maddy, cos no-one knows him from Adam. But somehow he knows where to look, spots me da and looks away, says something in Auntie's ear, and then the two of them start pushing a way slowly arm in arm through the crowd until the two men are facing each other at about twenty or thirty paces, like in Uncle's favourite movie *High Noon*, close enough to blow each other away.

The crowd doesn't notice, the music plays on and people dance. But for me the world's come to a stop and there's only silence and me sick da and angry uncle and the space between.

Da stares at him, not exactly hate, definitely not love, bit of both and something in between. Uncle stares back much the same, and again looks away, thinking whatever he's thinking.

The brothers stared,
Eyes of lead.
Each one fired,
Got hit in the head.
Both fell
Dead!

For a moment nothing happens, and I'm thinking we could be standing here in twenty years' time – I'll be in me thirties then and never attended secondary school.

It's me da who makes the first move. Leaves the shelter of the doorway and walks hands in pockets up to his older brother and stops. It happens quickly then, no guns, no punches. 'Hello, Grace.'

'Hello, Eddie,' answers Auntie.

'Hello, Maddy,' goes Da.

Uncle gives the smallest nod in history.

A kiss for Auntie and the brothers shake hands.

'Care to look around?' says Da.

'Thanks, but no thanks,' says Uncle.

'Or leave your car in for a service? I hear it's a little rusty.'

'You heard wrong. It's never been better.'

Me heart's pounding. At least they're talking.

Then a big sigh from Da and I distinctly hear him murmur, just loud enough for his brother, 'It's just that . . . I don't know how you're fixed, but, um . . .'

'What?'

'I might be needing someone to come in with me.'

Uncle Maddy looks at me da. I'm afraid he's going to hit him.

'I'm dead serious, Maddy,' says Da. 'I can't run this show on me own. We've had hatred in our hearts long enough. I'm tired of being your enemy. I want to give friendship a try.'

Uncle Maddy's shocked. Couldn't be more surprised if the Pope stepped out of his chopper and asked him to be Archbishop.

What a party that was! I wake up in the morning still dizzy with it, and I'm still buzzing when Slugs knocks for me. His uniform's ten sizes too big, mine's ten sizes too small, I don't know why we don't swap. He looks like a garden gnome, I look like a bunch of bolted broccoli. Not surprised Geri May won't walk with us.

I may look like an eejit who got out of bed and fell forty foot off a cliff, but I'm feeling good – not the old Hopper any more, not Hopper the Headcase but Hopper the Hero. I don't think

I'm quite done with bank robberies and intergalactic battles, but this feels like a new, hipper Hopper, walking easier and not so wired. I meet old faces and they all look the same, but me, I'm changed. I met an African and saved me daddy's garage.

Next month I'll be thirteen, and Da's hiring a space rocket to fly us to the Lunar DisneyWorld they've just opened. Well, actually, no, we're all piling into a couple of cabs and going out for a slap-up meal in town: Mam and Da, Auntie Gracie and Uncle Maddy, me and Fifi, Peach and Ambo, and Geri May of course – the whole crazy gang. It's still a long way off, but already I'm worrying it's all going to go wrong – Peach will insult Fifi and he'll walk out, or Da and Uncle Maddy will get their lines crossed and end up slugging it out in the street, or I'll lose the run of meself and try and kiss Geri May and get a smack in the moosh.

Auntie puts an arm round me.

'Don't worry, pet, it'll be a great night, a real celebration. Everybody will be on their best behaviour, and I prophesy with my little eye that your cousin Geri May will sit next to you all night. Now have a good day in school, pet.'

Auntie's right, and from now on, every time I get meself into a state, I'm gonna stop for a sec and close me eyes and go, *Si abotre* – take it easy.

THE BOTTLE-TOP KING
Jonathan Kebbe

Beware the sting of the bottle-top king!

Respect. That's what Lewis wants from his classmates. Nicknamed *Useless Lewis* or *Loo Brush*, he's fed up that he can't pluck up the nerve to join the drama club – and fed up that the only football he gets to play is pretend matches with his collection of bottle-tops at home.

Then Lewis's gangly mate Zulfi puts together a team for a five-a-side charity tournament. And he want *Lewis* to play! Can the bottle-top king burst out of his timid little shell and show everyone the hero inside?

A fresh, deliciously humorous story of a down-trodden pipsqueak who knows deep down he is a *genius*!

ISBN 0 440 864674

A YEARLING ORIGINAL PAPERBACK

JOEY PIGZA SWALLOWED THE KEY
Jack Gantos

'I think my brain is filled with bees.'

Joey is a good kid, maybe even a great kid, but he's always buzzing. As unpredictable as an unexploded bomb, he ricochets round the kitchen and spins down the school hall. He sharpens his finger in the pencil-sharpener and swallows his house key. He can't sit still for more than a minute – Joey is *wired*!

Told from Joey's own unique viewpoint by acclaimed American author Jack Gantos, this is an exceptionally funny and touching story.

'Funny, sad and very moving' *Jacqueline Wilson*

'Its wit, verve and strong story make it a fascinating read' *TES*

'An extraordinary book: moving, intensely funny and wonderfully enlightening' *English and Media magazine*

CORGI YEARLING BOOKS

ISBN 0 440 86433X